SIN OF
DAMNATION

More Warhammer 40,000 from Black Library

DARK IMPERIUM
Guy Haley

EISENHORN: XENOS
Dan Abnett

GAUNT'S GHOSTS:
THE FOUNDING OMNIBUS
Dan Abnett

CADIA STANDS
Justin D Hill

THE TALON OF HORUS
Aaron Dembski-Bowden

CRUSADE
Andy Clark

ASSAULT ON BLACK REACH
Nick Kyme

THE DEVASTATION OF BAAL
Guy Haley

ASHES OF PROSPERO
Gav Thorpe

WAR OF SECRETS
Phil Kelly

SIN OF DAMNATION

GAV THORPE

BLACK LIBRARY

For Richard Haliwell

A BLACK LIBRARY PUBLICATION

Sin of Damnation first published as *Space Hulk: The Novel*
in Great Britain in 2009 by Black Library.
'Sanguis Irae' first published in 2014.
This edition published in Great Britain in 2018 by
Black Library,
Games Workshop Ltd.,
Willow Road,
Nottingham, NG7 2WS, UK.

10 9 8 7 6 5 4 3 2 1

Produced by Games Workshop in Nottingham.
Cover illustration by Jon Cave.

Sin of Damnation © Copyright Games Workshop Limited 2018.
Sin of Damnation, GW, Games Workshop, Black Library, The
Horus Heresy, The Horus Heresy Eye logo, Space Marine, 40K,
Warhammer, Warhammer 40,000, the 'Aquila' Double-headed
Eagle logo, and all associated logos, illustrations, images, names,
creatures, races, vehicles, locations, weapons, characters, and the
distinctive likenesses thereof, are either ® or TM, and/or © Games
Workshop Limited, variably registered around the world.
All Rights Reserved.

A CIP record for this book is available from the British Library.

ISBN 13: 978-1-78496-748-2

No part of this publication may be reproduced, stored in a retrieval
system, or transmitted in any form or by any means, electronic,
mechanical, photocopying, recording or otherwise, without the
prior permission of the publishers.

This is a work of fiction. All the characters and events portrayed
in this book are fictional, and any resemblance to real people or
incidents is purely coincidental.

See Black Library on the internet at

blacklibrary.com

Find out more about Games Workshop
and the worlds of Warhammer 40,000 at

games-workshop.com

Printed and bound by CPI Group (UK) Ltd, Croydon, CR0 4YY

It is the 41st millennium. For more than a hundred centuries the Emperor has sat immobile on the Golden Throne of Earth. He is the Master of Mankind by the will of the gods, and master of a million worlds by the might of His inexhaustible armies. He is a rotting carcass writhing invisibly with power from the Dark Age of Technology. He is the Carrion Lord of the Imperium for whom a thousand souls are sacrificed every day, so that he may never truly die.

Yet even in his deathless state, the Emperor continues His eternal vigilance. Mighty battlefleets cross the daemon-infested miasma of the warp, the only route between distant stars, their way lit by the Astronomican, the psychic manifestation of the Emperor's will. Vast armies give battle in His name on uncounted worlds. Greatest amongst His soldiers are the Adeptus Astartes, the Space Marines, bioengineered super-warriors. Their comrades in arms are legion: the Astra Militarum and countless planetary defence forces, the ever-vigilant Inquisition and the tech-priests of the Adeptus Mechanicus to name only a few. But for all their multitudes, they are barely enough to hold off the ever-present threat from aliens, heretics, mutants — and worse.

To be a man in such times is to be one amongst untold billions. It is to live in the cruellest and most bloody regime imaginable. These are the tales of those times. Forget the power of technology and science, for so much has been forgotten, never to be re-learned. Forget the promise of progress and understanding, for in the grim dark future there is only war. There is no peace amongst the stars, only an eternity of carnage and slaughter, and the laughter of thirsting gods.

CONTENTS

SIN OF DAMNATION

MISSION TIME POST-IMPACT:

00.04.36

Darkness clung to the corroding bulkheads, thick and heavy with menace. Creaks and groans of contorting metal vied with the hiss of ancient pneumatics and drips from broken pipes. Something new and harsh broke the gloom and quiet of distant millennia: the metallic clump of heavy boots and star-bright rays of suit lamps.

Five huge figures strode purposefully through the confines of the derelict space hulk: Squad Lorenzo of the Blood Angels First Company. They were Terminators, the best of the elite Space Marines. All of them were giants, standing nearly three metres tall in their armour. Each a prized artefact, these armoured suits were the heaviest worn by any soldier of the Imperium, made of layers of titanium and ceramite capable of withstanding the most punishing damage. In the freezing vacuum of space or the boiling depths of a volcano, the Terminators were the deadliest warriors of the Adeptus Astartes, their skill and courage proven over centuries of battle. They came expecting victory.

'Containment underway,' Sergeant Lorenzo reported. The idle chatter of the squad had died away as they had neared the enemy. All were now intent upon the mission.

'The Blood Angels have returned,' Captain Raphael's voice crackled in Lorenzo's ear. The signal was somewhat distorted, having been broadcast more than a thousand kilometres, from where the force commander monitored events aboard the orbiting strike cruiser *Angel's Sword*. 'For six centuries we have carried the burden of defeat, the stigma of failure. Now we redeem ourselves.'

Eighty Terminators of the Blood Angels were establishing a foothold aboard the space hulk. Their mission was simple: eradicate the alien threat. Several hundred metres behind Squad Lorenzo a cordon of veteran warriors guarded the impact site, where Techmarines and other support was being established. When all was ready they would advance on their foes. For the moment, however, Lorenzo and his warriors were out on their own.

The squad had been tasked with destroying the controls of a still-active bank of saviour pods. If the enemy were allowed to escape the space hulk aboard the lifeboats their infection could spread to other ships and distant worlds. That could not be allowed to happen. Such was the importance of containment, Lorenzo's squad were considered expendable.

Heralded by the glare of their armour lights, the Space Marines advanced in single file along a winding concourse. The warriors' suits of Tactical Dreadnought armour filled the narrow corridor, their massive shoulder pads occasionally scraping the metal walls. Their red livery shone bright in the light of the lamps, a declaration of fearlessness and determination. The Blood Angels did not fight in the shadows.

The Terminators stomped forwards accompanied by the growl of servos and wheezing of fibre-bundles from their suits. At their head, Lorenzo's sensorium showed that the maze of corridors ahead was deserted. He adjusted the range to three hundred metres and caught his breath when the glowing image on his auto-senses tinged with a smudge of green at the limit of the sensor's range. He waited several seconds, but the image did not resolve into movement. The enemy were dormant.

'Section secure, pattern thetos,' the sergeant said, thumbing the activation stud on his sword.

The blade hummed into life, the actinic blue of its power field bathing the corridor with flickering light. In the double-circle glare of Lorenzo's armour lamps, the corridor was laid bare. The latticed decking was warped in places but unbroken, while the walls that lined the narrow passageway were made of bolted metal sheets corroded and pitted with decay. The only sound was the buzz of the power weapon, tramping boots and the wheeze of powered armour as the rest of the squad moved up into position behind their sergeant.

The sensorium signal still had not changed and Lorenzo advanced, bringing his storm bolter up to the firing position. He checked the magazine readout in his display: thirty-two rounds.

'Detecting an energy wave from starboard, brother-sergeant,' Valencio announced. 'Indeterminate distance. Possibly a cable or generator.'

'Not of mission significance,' said Lorenzo, slowing as he approached a junction with another corridor coming from the right. 'Continue to advance.'

Swinging around, the beams of his lamps swaying across the walls, Lorenzo stared down the corridor and took two steps forward. Even with the suit lights, visibility was poor. Motes of rust and flaking paint drifted down from the ceiling and the contorted walls of the passage created strange shadows. Lorenzo scanned the scene looking for openings, his breathing calm, his mind focussed. The new passageway had two doors ahead: one on the right a dozen metres forward, another on the left thirty metres away. Deino strode across the junction behind the sergeant, his weapon covering the other approach.

'Command deck, update on tactical mapping,' Lorenzo said.

The comm buzzed for several seconds before the voice of one of the strike cruiser's bridge technicians arrived in Lorenzo's ear.

'Nearly complete,' the crewman said. 'Transmitting data over link now.'

Lorenzo's helmet display fuzzed blue for a second and then resolved into a clearer image as the scan data from the strike cruiser fused with the auto-senses of his armoured suit. A wire frame schematic was imposed over his vision and at a sub-vocal command an independent map appeared in his right eye. In places the map was indistinct or absent, the scanners of the strike cruiser unable to penetrate for some as-yet unknown reason. Lorenzo looked over the layout of the surrounding rooms and corridors, whilst maintaining a vigilant gaze on the sensorium data with his other eye. The contact echoes still had not moved. The energy spike reported by Valencio was some distance away and of no importance.

'Egress location now marked,' a serf aboard the strike cruiser reported. Moments later the helmet display flickered as it updated itself. A blinking icon of a skull drew Lorenzo's attention to a room some eighty metres ahead. This was the saviour pod control room, the squad's objective. Lorenzo had been tasked with destroying the launch mechanisms, ensuring that their alien prey could not escape the hulk. It was standard combat doctrine: contain and annihilate.

From the map, Lorenzo could also see that the branch he was on led to a subset of rooms isolated from the main thoroughfare they were following. Sensorium data was blank and Lorenzo needed to know if there was an ingress route on their flank. Dozens of metres behind the squad more Terminators were setting up a defensive cordon around the breaching zone, but out here beyond the perimeter there were any number of ways the squad might be surrounded.

'Valencio and Zael, with me,' Lorenzo commanded. 'Search and secure. Deino and Goriel, flank protection.'

Lorenzo strode forwards once more. Zael fell in behind the sergeant, the igniter of his heavy flamer sparking and stuttering. Valencio brought up the rear, keeping the standard five metre clearance.

Stopping two metres beyond the first door, Lorenzo settled into overwatch stance, legs braced, targeter set to wide focus. Behind him Zael turned and faced the door. Deactivating the field on his power fist, the Terminator flicked the door lever. With a screech, the door shuddered open halfway and then squealed to a stop. Zael grabbed the door's edge and hauled it sideways, his powered actuators pushing the door into its wall cavity with more shrieking protests from the ancient metal. Inside his helmet, the Terminator grimaced at the sound.

The room beyond was square, less than ten metres to a wall, and a further door lay open on the opposite side. Cracked tiles paved the floor, thick with grime. The walls had been crudely whitewashed at some point in the distant centuries but were now bare metal except for the odd patch of peeling paint.

'Movement!' Goriel's sharp warning echoed in everyone's ear.

* * *

00.05.97

The greenish fuzz on the sensorium net was shifting, resolving into individual signatures. They were rapidly closing in on the Terminators' position. The clump split into two groups, spreading out to the left and right. Lorenzo counted seven distinct movements heading towards him and five others circling to the other side of Deino and Goriel. Neither group's course seemed to comply with the schematic data.

'Secure main corridor, continue sweep,' Lorenzo barked. 'Watch for entry points. Look for super- and sub-layer approaches.'

The sergeant pressed ahead towards the next door. Valencio followed, his gaze scanning left and right for breaches in the walls, floor and ceiling, checking that his sergeant's rear quarter was protected. At the back, Zael clumped across the room and stopped at the open doorway, his heavy flamer directed down the corridor beyond.

'Ceiling breach,' Zael reported as he caught sight of a gaping crack in a heavy pipe that ran half the length of the fifty-metre corridor before turning sharply into a bulkhead.

The contacts on the sensorium were less than seventy-five metres away from Lorenzo, and within fifty metres of Deino.

'Brothers, the enemy are at hand. Summon all of your resolve, and your animosity,' Lorenzo told his squad.

The sergeant reached the door and swung around to face it. It was also activated by the pull of a lever and hissed out of sight with less effort than the previous one. Lorenzo stepped forwards as soon as the door was open, allowing Valencio to continue his advance along the corridor.

From a corroded grating in the floor ahead of Deino something fast and agile sprang into the corridor. It leapt towards the Terminator on bounding legs, four whip-muscled arms clawing at the passage wall as it righted itself. It had a bulbous, purple head. The rest of its body was covered in a dark blue chitin. Its eyes glittered in the lamps of Deino's suit.

'Visual contact!' said Deino. 'Confirm contact: genestealer.'

The creature had taken only three strides along the corridor when Deino opened fire. The passage rang with the clamour of the storm bolter's roar. With alien quickness the thing leapt from one wall to the other, the Terminator's initial burst of fire ripping a trail of detonations across bare metal. Another shape emerged from the darkness as the first hurtled forward with a lithe gait, digging the claws of its upper arms into the floor to increase momentum.

Deino's second salvo caught the creature across the head and back, tearing bloody chunks from it. Thick blood splashed across the wall and floors. The second creature leapt over its fallen companion without hesitation and Deino fired again.

'Confirmed kill, multiple targets approaching,' Deino said calmly. He fired once more. 'Threat minimal.'

00.06.18

'Ingress!' announced Zael, squeezing the trigger on his heavy flamer. A sheet of fire roared along the corridor, bathing the ceiling and the pipe with promethium fury. Something flailed in the inferno, soundlessly spasming as the cleansing fires melted through its carapace, flesh and bones. Charred bodies fell from the destroyed pipework. The adhesive promethium clung to the walls, coating the corridor with white-hot flames.

'Cleanse and burn!' Zael's spirits soared as he saw the creatures incinerated.

'Hold stance!' ordered Lorenzo.

The staccato rhythm of Deino's storm bolter rang through

the corridors as he unloaded his weapon's magazine into the onrushing tide of creatures boiling up from a crawl-space beneath the decking. The crackle of Zael's heavy flamer sounded again as more creatures emerged in front of him.

The room Lorenzo found himself in was long and thin, with stone-lined walls carved with faint patterns. A vent in the far corner to his right blew out a steady stream of dust, which swirled through the beams of the sergeant's lights as he stepped forward. There were no other doors.

Lorenzo was about to turn away when he noticed that the dust from the vent had stopped.

00.06.25

A warning tone sounded and one of the signals on the sensorium flashed red: imminent threat. A moment later the vent cover was smashed out and one of the aliens was propelling itself through the air towards Lorenzo. With no time to fire, the sergeant brought his power sword up to a parry position, slicing through an outstretched claw. The genestealer's three other clawed hands gouged furrows across Lorenzo's helmet and right shoulder guard, knocking him backwards a step.

'Blood of Baal!' spat Lorenzo as he lashed the power sword into the creature's head, splitting it from cheek to neck in a fountain of gore.

A reflexive paroxysm caused the creature to snap its arms shut, clamping onto Lorenzo's right arm, talons scratching at the outer ceramite layer of the sergeant's armour. With a grunt, he smashed the body away with his storm bolter.

He looked down at the bloodied thing sprawled on the floor. It twitched with some vestigial remnants of life, despite its grievous wounds. Memories six hundred years old surfaced in the sergeant's mind, images of the Blood Angels aboard another space hulk in a time that seemed an age ago. The beasts had taken a bloody toll in that campaign and the Blood Angels had teetered upon the precipice of annihilation. Lorenzo had been one of only fifty battle-brothers to survive the encounter. Those ashamed few had returned to Baal to lick their wounds like scolded curs.

Looking at the fanged monstrosity at his feet, Lorenzo felt a mixture of revulsion and shame, tinged with an almost unknown sensation: anxiety. Though he had fought gloriously for the Emperor for more than half a dozen centuries and across countless battle zones, the alien at his feet reminded Lorenzo of a time when he had been alone in the darkness. The Blood Angels had failed on that day and the stain of defeat hung heavily in Lorenzo's mind.

There was only one response to the emotions vying for control of Lorenzo's thoughts. Anger welled up inside him, a righteous ire fuelled by self-loathing and a deep hatred of the creatures he faced. The Blood Angels had been bloodied but not destroyed. They had taken the shame of failure into their hearts and nurtured it. Over the long years and decades they had taken the rough ore of weakness and beaten it with faith and resolve, honing it into a bright sword of admonition. From weakness came strength and from adversity came the desire to prevail. The sergeant raised an armoured boot and brought it down on the genestealer's head, crushing it to a pulp upon the floor. Thick blood oozed from under the Space Marine's magnetized sole and dribbled into the cracks between the tiles.

This time there would be no defeat, no retreat.

* * *

00.06.29

A shout over the comm and a blazing flash on the sensorium warned that Zael was in trouble. A wave of hazy blips was speeding down the corridor towards the Terminator. Valencio responded first, slewing his armour around and pounding back towards the first room.

'One burst left,' warned Zael.

'Save that for the objective,' order Lorenzo.

'Clear for shot!' snapped Valencio as he thundered into the room behind the heavy flamer-armed Space Marine.

Seven or eight of the creatures could be seen past the dancing flames left by Valencio's defensive fire. As the inferno burnt itself out, they rushed forwards, claws opened, dead eyes fixed on Zael. The Terminator took a step backwards and to one side, opening up Valencio's view of the corridor in front of him.

'Purge the xenos!' laughed Valencio as he opened fire, the storm of explosive bolts from his weapon sending heads and limbs flying as the shells detonated inside their targets. The controlled fire blew apart four of the aliens, one after the other. 'Did you see that, brother-sergeant? Four in one volley!'

With a sickening click and a kick that caused the storm bolter to shudder in Valencio's grip, the weapon stopped firing. A hazard message flickered into his helmet display: AMMUNITION FEED JAM.

'Mercy of the Angel...' Valencio muttered as three more genestealers sprinted down the corridor towards him.

00.06.38

Goriel had worked his way forward along a tunnel that ran parallel to Deino's position. A glance at the sensorium showed the bulk of contacts closing in on Zael and Valencio's

16

location. Boosting the power to his legs, the Terminator broke into an awkward run, his footfalls crashing along the metal decking as he pounded around a corner ahead.

The passage he was on intersected at a T-junction with the corridor covered by Valencio. In the glow thrown out by patches of flickering promethium Goriel saw one of the creatures coiling its muscles, ready to spring towards Valencio's location. Goriel fired on instinct, his storm bolter roaring before the conscious thought had entered his mind. The alien beast was thrown aside, its legs ripped away.

Another appeared at the junction ahead and bounded off the wall and around the corner, changing its direction of attack towards Goriel. It made no attempt to hide, relying on its breakneck speed to close the distance. The tactic failed as a slew of bolter rounds from Goriel's weapon blew apart its head and body.

'Jam cleared!' announced Valencio and a moment later the burning trails of bolter rounds sped past the junction and the *crump* of detonations sounded along the metallic maze.

'Push forward,' said Lorenzo. 'Regroup at grid point thirteen-delta.'

With Lorenzo and Goriel leading the way, the squad headed onwards into the darkness. The genestealers attacked haphazardly, dashing from the shadows and bursting from pipes and vents singly and in pairs. The disciplined fire of the Blood Angels easily cut them down. More blips on the sensorium showed that others were rapidly closing in on the Terminators' position.

As they came to a double cross junction, Valencio swung around and covered the rear while Goriel and Deino spread out to guard the other approaches. Lorenzo advanced towards the objective highlighted in his helm display, his storm bolter spitting rounds into a heavy door at the end of the corridor. The thumb-sized rockets tore apart the metal barrier, revealing the room beyond. Dimly lit screens glowed in the chamber atop banks of keyboards and buttons.

It was the launch control chamber for the saviour pods: the objective. The squad's orders were to destroy the controls beyond any hope of repair, ensuring that none of the lifeboats could be launched.

'Brother Zael, purify,' the sergeant said. He stepped into a side corridor as Zael readied his heavy flamer. Bursts of storm bolter fire from Goriel and Valencio announced the arrival of more enemies.

Promethium scorched into the launch room and glass-panelled data displays exploded. Sparks erupted from melting cables as Zael emptied the tank of his weapon. Thick black smoke poured from the room, billowing along the thermals created by the inferno, swathing the squad in gloom. Lorenzo's auto-senses flickered through the spectrum of options and settled on a heat-capture image. In the reflected glow of the burning control room, the sergeant could see through the smog as if it was not there. He stepped back into the corridor and analysed the damage done by Zael's flamer.

Metal cabinets had been reduced to slurry and molten gobbets of metal pinged and cooled on the rockcrete floor. Ancient circuits had been irreparably scorched and millennia-old pistons sagged like sodden paper.

'Control, objective complete,' Lorenzo announced.

'Affirmed,' a voice replied. 'Return to perimeter for orders.'

Lorenzo turned away from the control room and looked at the sensorium display. Green flickers warily circled ahead, growing in number. The genestealers were trapped aboard the space hulk with the Terminators. Now the true battle would begin.

It was several hundred metres back to the breach head, and dozens of foes now lay in front of the Terminators. Lorenzo ejected the magazine from his storm bolter and slammed in another.

'Vengeance shall be ours, my brothers.'

00.06.99

Nearly half a kilometre behind Lorenzo, Sergeant Gideon nodded to himself as he listened to the reports over the comm-net, his Terminator armour whining in protest as it failed to replicate the movement. All was proceeding as expected. The breaching zone was well established and the support and reserve units had moved on board. The veterans of the Blood Angels First Company were preparing to press onwards into the space hulk's depths.

'Squad Gideon, secure point eighty-omega,' Captain Raphael's orders came through terse and clipped. 'Prevent enemy reinforcements from passing the junction.'

'Affirmative, point eighty-omega,' replied Gideon. 'Attack pattern diablo, advance.'

He raised the thunder hammer in his right hand and signalled for his squad to move out. Scipio took the point position, his storm bolter raised and ready. Brother Leon fell in behind him, the six barrels of his assault cannon rotating slowly as if in anticipation of the battle to come. Gideon stepped into position next, Omnio not far behind. Noctis brought up the back of the short column, turning occasionally to cover the approach to the rear.

'Has it been confirmed that these are the same creatures that were encountered before?' asked Scipio.

'Lorenzo and the other survivors are convinced,' said Gideon. 'That's good enough for me.'

'Truly we have been blessed with this opportunity for vengeance,' said Scipio.

'They are the same *species* of alien,' Omnio clarified. 'Not the actual life forms our predecessors encountered.'

'Good enough for me,' said Scipio. He swayed to the left and pointed to an alcove in the wall. 'Possible entry point.'

Leon's assault cannon swung towards the offending space but the alcove was devoid of any hole or other route of attack. The Terminator grunted in disappointment and continued after Scipio.

'It is hard to believe these are Ymgarlian genestealers,' said Scipio. 'So many creatures from such a small moon.'

'It does raise some difficult questions about our understanding of the genestealer species,' admitted Omnio. 'But as the Angel once said, "There are more things in the darkness than man can ever count". It is arrogance to presume we know everything.'

'We should torpedo the entire hulk and be done,' said Noctis as he rejoined the back of the squad from where he had been standing rearguard.

'That would be an opportunity missed,' said Omnio. 'Some of these vessels might be Dark Age. Who can say what secrets they hide?'

'And what dangers,' added Gideon. 'Keep vigilant.'

The squad had advanced the perimeter by some two hundred metres. Roughly the same distance ahead a cloud of contacts was registering on the Terminators' scanners. At this distance it was impossible to discern individual life forms, but Gideon estimated there to be a hundred or more. They were moving, but not in any purposeful sense that he could recognise.

Gideon pushed the squad onwards. They came upon a tangled mess of gantries and chambers where the hulls of two ships had been compacted together by the strange tides of the warp. Like a fault line in a planet's bedrock, the line between the two ships was clear and distinct. An unidentifiable rock-like material replaced metal and the colours changed from greys and silvers to greens and blues. Doorways were wider and higher and the distorted walls and floors allowed more space for the Terminators. Gideon picked up the pace, aware that every moment before the squad was in position was an opportunity for the Blood Angels' alien adversaries to attack the perimeter.

'Command to all squads, mission update,' announced Captain Raphael. 'Cyber-Altered Task unit deployed for deep recon. Enemy force estimate now at excess of forty thousand. Ninety-five per cent dormancy and falling. Remember your fallen forebrothers and fight with honour.'

'Angel's mercy, that's a lot of targets,' said Scipio.

'Enough to go around,' said Leon.

'Leon, move ahead and cover the junction,' Gideon ordered, ignoring the squad's chatter. 'Noctis, take up flank protection position to Leon's left. The rest of you, disperse pattern deimos, guard the approaches.'

On the sergeant's command the squad split, each warrior disappearing into the darkness to take up his assigned position. Having extended the breach head by another three hundred metres, they settled into overwatch and awaited the enemy. On the sensorium, the green blurs separated into distinct signatures as the foe converged on Squad Gideon from three directions.

00.07.12

There was movement right at the edge of the light from Leon's suit lamps and he resisted the urge to open fire. The motor of his assault cannon growled like a beast ready to pounce and Leon waited expectantly for a clear target. The sensorium showed a score or more of creatures in the darkness of the tunnels ahead. They circled for a short while, seeking some other route towards the Blood Angels' positions. Evidently this endeavour met with failure. One moment the corridor was empty, the next a horde of blue and purple bodies hurtled along its length towards Leon like water bursting through a hole in a dam.

He opened fire, the barrels of the assault cannon rotating up to speed in a heartbeat, a torrent of shells screaming down the passageway in another. Leon's auto-senses had kicked in the audio dampeners the moment he had pressed the trigger, but even through the immense plasteel plates armouring his body the Terminator could feel the concussive shockwave that filled the room.

In a two-second burst half a dozen creatures were shredded, their bodies vaporised by the fusillade. Leon paused for a moment, allowing his weapon's barrels and motors to cool, and then opened fire again. Each devastating burst obliterated everything in front of the Terminator.

Virtually hypnotised by the carnage he was wreaking, Leon almost failed to notice a group of sensorium contacts moving down a corridor parallel to the one he was covering. He began to back away from the door to the room, giving himself more time to fire. He was too slow. With a scream of rending metal and a clang, the genestealers smashed through a door just around a corner ahead and within a second they were inside the room with Leon.

'Die!' he bellowed, unleashing the fury of his assault cannon in one long burst. Tracing an arc with his weapon, Leon cut down the first swathe of attackers, but more were following quickly in their wake. The trigger still locked down, Leon turned the blaze of shells upon the next wave of aliens. Fire and gore and splinters from the ruined walls filled the corridor for a moment.

With an explosion that hurled Leon from his feet, the assault cannon's barrels burst. The white-hot metal scythed into his armour, leaving steaming shreds of alloy smoking across his shoulder and helm. Clawed hands and feet gouged further rents in his suit as the beasts streamed through the room. One blow caught a plasteel-sheathed cable under Leon's left arm, paralysing his armour on that side and rendering his power fist inert.

'Point position down!' he snarled over the comm as the genestealers raced past. There was nothing else he could do.

00.08.04

'Time to prove yourselves once again, my friends,' Gideon muttered to his thunder hammer and storm shield, Leon's warning still ringing in his ears. 'Destroy your foe and protect your bearer!'

He and Omnio had linked up and had moved towards Leon's position when the first attack had begun. Their only hope of holding back the growing tide of aliens was a bottleneck up ahead, where the twisted plascrete tunnels converged into a single room.

The room itself was barely fifteen metres wide, the walls heavily pitted and cracked. It had been some kind of pumping station in a past age. Broken pipes jutted from the angle of wall and ceiling. Globulous strings of thick fluid hung from their shattered ends and occasionally dripped into oily puddles at the base of the walls. The remnants of ancient valves and wheels seized with rust covered the ceiling.

Omnio positioned himself facing the open door, opposite

the predicted approach of the enemy, storm bolter loaded and aimed. Gideon waited to one side of his squad-brother, ready to step forward and attack should any creature get past Omnio's fire.

It was not long before the first genestealer appeared, dropping down from a shattered duct in the ceiling of the corridor ahead. It was up and running in a moment, spring-jointed legs pumping fast as it sprinted towards the Terminators. Its claws raked chips of stone from the tiles underfoot. The alien's eyes shone in the dull yellow glow of ancient lightstrips. There was no emotion in that gaze, only the lethal intent of a predator.

'Maybe it isn't as illogical as I first thought,' Omnio said, firing a brief burst down the corridor.

'What's that?' said Gideon.

'You, carrying that hammer... and shield even... though you're no longer... in an assault squad,' explained Omnio, pausing every few words to open fire. 'In close confines... such as these, the added... potential at close quarters, when... combined with a ranged weapon-armed comrade... provides a tactical advantage... not possible by the standard sergeant's wargear.'

Gideon snorted.

'Tactical advantage?' said the sergeant, raising the large hammer and shield to a guard posture. 'I carry these weapons to honour my armour.'

'How so?' asked Omnio, still firing, his attention fixed on the aliens running and leaping out of the room at the far end of the passageway.

'When I first transferred to sergeant, I abandoned my trusted friends here for the traditional sword and storm bolter,' said Gideon. 'In the next battle, a stray shot from an ork penetrated the sub-thorax pipes and immobilised my left leg. I know when my armour is telling me something. I've carried these since.'

'A wise m–' Omnio's reply was cut short as a genestealer launched itself through the door, having scuttled its way along the ceiling of the corridor. With incredible speed, twisting in the air, it landed on Omnio, sword-like claws sending up shards of ceramite from the Terminator's breastplate. Omnio lurched backwards under the impact, the artificial muscles of his armour straining but holding firm.

Gideon stepped forwards and brought his thunder hammer down onto the creature's back. The power field around the hammer's head exploded in a blue flash as the blow landed. Spine shattered, carapace cracked, the genestealer flopped to the stone floor like a grounded fish.

Gideon had no time to admire his deadly handiwork. Two more aliens were in the room, claws outstretched, fanged jaws gaping. The first lunged for the sergeant. Gideon brought up his storm shield to ward off its attacks. A flare of energy illuminated the room and the genestealer was hurled into the wall. The other beast ducked beneath the swing of the sergeant's hammer and, with a jarring screech of chitin on metal, punched two sets of its claws into Omnio's leg.

The alien that had been repulsed by Gideon's storm shield sprang forwards again, one arm hanging loosely at its side. Even wounded it was astoundingly fast, dodging Gideon's block with his shield, yet not so skilful that it could avoid the thunder hammer aimed towards it. In one sweep the glowing weapon smashed the creature's head clean off.

Omnio toppled to one side, the reinforced struts inside his leg armour buckling under the pressure of the genestealer's powerful grip. The Terminator grabbed an arm in his power fist and yanked it from the socket, yellow ichor spraying across his armour. Fist shimmering with energy, Omnio dug his fingers point first into the genestealer's neck, snapping vertebrae. As the genestealer twitched in its death throes, Omnio tried to prise off the creature's corpse but only succeeded in mashing it into small lumps with his power fist. The genestealer's claws had jammed the knee joint in his leg. To all intents and purposes, the Terminator was now immobilised.

'Combat potential negated,' Omnio announced disconsolately. 'I need a Techmarine.'

Gideon stepped protectively between his fallen battle-brother and the doorway, thunder hammer ready. On his sensorium, more blips raced towards the room.

00.09.56

A genestealer ducked into a side corridor before Lorenzo could open fire. The one behind it was not so fortunate and the sergeant blew it to pieces with a burst from his storm bolter. Checking his sensorium, Lorenzo noted that their foe was approaching more cautiously than before. They gathered in small groups out of sight and then launched themselves at the Terminators in short waves. Though it showed more intelligence than the suicidal charges the genestealers had been employing in the first phase of the battle, the tactic was still crude and easily countered.

Lorenzo suppressed a moment of unease as he recalled the massed attacks of the genestealers during his last encounter with them. On that occasion they had gathered in their hundreds, clawing and leaping over their fallen to overwhelm the Blood Angels with sheer weight of numbers. So far only a small fraction of the foe was awake, but Lorenzo knew that as more rose from their hibernation the attacks would get deadlier.

Despite the sergeant's concerns, none of the aliens had yet broken through the cordon of Squad Lorenzo, though the Terminators were expending a considerable amount of ammunition to defend their positions. The Techmarines had resupplied the squad once already, but Zael had reported his heavy flamer tank was half-full and the rest of the squad each had only a few magazines remaining.

The next supply run was due in three minutes. Lorenzo knew other squads were being pressed harder elsewhere along the line and resisted the urge to request that their own re-equip be brought forward.

'Squad Lorenzo, this is command.' Captain Raphael's voice was calm and measured, though Lorenzo could guess at the many decisions straining his attention. 'C.A.T. signal is erratic, information upload incomplete. I need you to physically locate the unit and retrieve it for data analysis. Squad Gideon will join from omega grid, co-ordinate the search with Sergeant Gideon.'

'Affirmative, brother-captain,' Lorenzo responded. 'Last known C.A.T. position?'

'Somewhere in theta grid, directly ahead of your location,' the captain told him. 'Transmitting frequency signature to sensorium net.'

The display superimposed onto Lorenzo's vision flickered as the update came through. A haze of flashing red appeared over the map layout some fifty metres from where he was. Somewhere in the sprawl of corridors ahead, the Cyber-Altered Task unit was wandering in circles. Having been teleported into the heart of the space hulk for deep scans and reconnaissance, the automated unit was evidently malfunctioning or damaged. The data it had collected was essential to Captain Raphael and the C.A.T. needed to be recovered quickly.

'Frequency locked in, brother-captain,' Lorenzo told his commander.

'Acknowledged,' came the captain's static-clouded reply. 'We pursue our own, sublime goal. We seek vindication.'

'In the name of the Angel and for the honour of Baal,' Lorenzo responded and the link fell silent. He switched to squad broadcast. 'Advance pattern majestic. Gideon and his squad approaching from ahead, so watch your fire.'

'We'll get there first,' Valencio said as he moved to the head of the squad. 'The honour shall be ours.'

The newest member of Squad Lorenzo lumbered onto a contorted walkway that crossed over a dormant generator plant. Nothing stirred in the blackness below and the sensorium displayed no contacts within twenty metres. Not trusting the corroded metal to take the weight of more than one Terminator, Lorenzo waited until Valencio was on the steps at the other side of the chamber before waving Zael forwards. One by one they crossed the artificial ravine while Valencio provided covering fire from the room beyond.

As he descended the steps, Lorenzo could see Valencio silhouetted by the muzzle flare of his storm bolter, his shadow cast sharply across the debris-littered floor with each burst. Entering the room beyond the stairway, Lorenzo added his fire to that of Valencio, gunning down a handful of genestealers as they hurtled into the chamber. For a moment all was din and confusion, brought to an abrupt end by a sheet of fire from Zael's heavy flamer. Unearthly screeches sounded the genestealers' demise, the first sound he had heard them utter. The sudden quiet that descended was broken only by the sound of flames, the pings and cracks of cooling metal and the whistle of superheated blood steaming from the aliens' corpses.

The next passageway was clear of foes and Valencio advanced quickly, reaching a T-junction at its end while the rest of the squad filed into the room, burnt carcasses crunching underfoot. Now closer to the signal of the C.A.T., Lorenzo could see that the automaton was somewhere in the network of tunnels less than thirty metres ahead. The signal was moving erratically, its transmission reflected and echoed by the distorted walls of the hulk.

'Valencio, Deino, sweep right,' the sergeant ordered. 'Zael and Goriel, follow my lead.'

Thus split, the squad made their way into the rat's nest of collapsed corridors, stairwells, rooms and ducts. Their suit lamps blazing, they cast their sharp eyes into broken vents and under fallen workstations, seeking the task unit. Quickly and methodically, the squad homed in on their objective, their search occasionally punctuated by a burst of storm bolter fire as a lone genestealer sprang from the shadows.

'C.A.T. located,' announced Goriel.

Lorenzo fixed on his battle-brother's identification contact. He shouldered his way through tangles of twisted metal and clambered over rubble heaps to forge a way to the recon device. The sergeant found Goriel and Zael in a domed hall at the centre of three radiating corridors. Goriel held the C.A.T. in his deactivated power fist.

The Cyber-Altered Task unit was a tracked automaton about half a metre in length, studded with sensor spurs and data-aerials. Jointed metallic limbs splayed from its central hull and wiggled forlornly in Goriel's grasp. At the end of a prehensile cable, a gilded skull containing the C.A.T.'s metriculator waggled left and right as it continued its scans. Its red eyes glowed and dimmed as it processed the data while its tracks whirred back and forth as the C.A.T. struggled to get free.

'Salutations, brethren,' said Valencio, entering from the opposite side of the hall. 'It seems Goriel has found a new friend.'

'Take it,' Goriel said, thrusting the C.A.T. towards Valencio. 'You seem the motherly type.'

The glow around Valencio's chainfist vanished as he cut off the power supply. Delicately, he took the shuddering cyber-scout from Goriel and held it up so that its scanner lenses were pointed towards his face.

'Don't fret, little friend,' Valencio said in a hushed voice, a hint of a laugh in his tone. 'Brother Goriel is just being sour. I'll look after you.'

Lorenzo was about to admonish the pair for the light-hearted behaviour when a squad-to-squad transmission cut across the comm.

'Lorenzo, this is Gideon,' a voice crackled in the sergeant's ear. 'Can you hear me?'

'I can,' Lorenzo replied. 'And most welcome it is.'

'Don't thank me just yet,' Gideon said. 'We are approaching your position, one hundred and fifty metres on your left flank. There is a large concentration of sensorium contacts in grid medusa, just out of your range, growing more active. They'll be on you before we arrive.'

'Thank you for the warning, Gideon,' said Lorenzo. He consulted the sensorium map. 'Rendezvous at theta-four and we'll return to the perimeter in force.'

'Affirmative, Lorenzo,' said Gideon. 'May the Angel guide your fury and the Emperor guard your backs.'

'Praise Sanguinius,' Lorenzo intoned. 'Deino and Zael, cleanse towards theta-four. We will escort the C.A.T. Confirm?'

The two Terminators signalled back their compliance, their signature blips moving away on the sensorium. Lorenzo led the other group, the rear guarded by Goriel, with Valencio sandwiched protectively between. They had advanced only a dozen metres when the leading edge of the genestealer contacts reported by Gideon showed on the sensorium. There were at least twenty of the aliens, and more appeared on the scanner over the next few seconds.

'Contact!' Deino shouted over the comm. A moment later gunfire echoed dully around the labyrinth of corridors, the sound distant and distorted.

The way ahead was tortuous, with blast doors sealing off many routes and fallen ceilings blocking others. Rooms that showed up as empty on the sensorium scan were filled with impassable debris and walkways were bent and broken. On the scanner, Zael and Deino were no more than fifteen metres away, but in the wreckage of the hulk's depths Lorenzo could see no sign of them, or any way to move further forward.

'Clear a path,' Lorenzo told Valencio as the sergeant fell in behind Goriel.

'As the Angel, I shall lead the way,' laughed Valencio. He hooked his storm bolter to his belt and took the C.A.T. in his right hand. His left hand now free, he powered up his chainfist.

Chainfist blades whirring and blazing, Valencio punched his way through a plascrete wall, showering himself with dust and shards. He stepped into the darkness beyond, his further progress accompanied by the screech of tortured metal and the thud of exploding plascrete slabs.

Goriel followed next, Lorenzo turning to stand sentry at the makeshift passage battered through the debris by Valencio. More than a dozen genestealers were closing fast, coming up from the hallway where the squad had just been. Glancing left, right and above, Lorenzo realised the corridor was broken in many places and allowed far too many access points to defend with any confidence. Stepping backwards, storm bolter held ready to fire, the sergeant followed Valencio and Goriel along the tangled pathway.

A hideous purple face appeared at the ragged entrance a few seconds after Lorenzo had begun his withdrawal. The sergeant opened fire immediately, two rounds scattering the genestealer's brains and skull into the darkness. Another alien appeared and Lorenzo gunned it down, taking another step backwards. With agonising slowness, the sergeant backed along the cleared path, unleashing a salvo of fire every couple of seconds as more and more genestealers poured into the breach after him. Between the roars of his storm bolter, Lorenzo caught other bursts of fire echoing from behind him. A glance at the sensorium showed that Gideon's squad was not far behind. Through a gap in the tangled girders and joists, the sergeant saw licks of fire: Zael's flamer. Heartened, Lorenzo emptied the magazine on his storm bolter, gunning down five aliens in the long salvo, and then turned and broke into a run.

The sergeant didn't need to check his sensorium to know that the genestealers were barely ten metres behind him; his sharp ears and armour's auto-senses picked up the scratching of claws and sharp hisses at his back.

Lorenzo thundered into a wide, low room filled with ruined databank consoles. Just as he broke into the dim green light something smashed into the back of his armour. Pitching forward, his armour's fibre bundles and motors shrieked in their fight to keep him balanced, but lost. He stumbled to one knee, desperately trying to reach behind him with his power sword. A clawed hand appeared in his vision and then something inhumanly strong smashed into the back of the sergeant's helm, stunning him.

* * *

00.11.67

Deino heard rather than saw Sergeant Lorenzo, a cacophonic clattering of armour and shattering tiles. His blood thundering in his ears, time seemed to slow down for Deino. Turning left towards the sound, the Terminator raised his storm bolter to shoulder height and flicked the single-fire switch. Lorenzo was down on one knee, a genestealer perched on his back, its foot claws gripping the exhaust vents of the sergeant's armour, both pairs of foreclaws seizing his helm, trying to twist off his head.

The aiming reticule in Deino's right eye danced around the genestealer as the alien swayed backwards and forwards, trying to lever Lorenzo's head from his shoulders. Deino didn't wait for the lock-on. His eyes were more accurate than any metriculator. He took a deep breath and fired.

'Blessed be the sure of shot for they shall bring vengeance,' Deino whispered as the bolt roared from the muzzle, its rocket punching it forward. A moment later the bolt penetrated the genestealer's left eye and the mass-reactive warhead detonated, splitting apart the creature's head. Lorenzo tried to right himself and another alien appeared from the hole smashed through the wall by Valencio. Deino fired again.

'Praise to the Angel for he shall guide my aim,' he whispered while the bolt pierced the creature's chest and then exploded in a shower of chitin and ribs. Four more genestealers leapt through the gap and each was felled in turn by a round from Deino's weapon, the shots accompanied by a litany of accuracy spilling from the Space Marine's lips.

A Terminator in the heraldry of Gideon's squad loomed over Lorenzo, an assault cannon connected to his right arm by heavy bolts and makeshift struts. A light-suppressing filter materialised over Deino's vision as Leon opened fire, saving the Terminator's eyes from the blinding muzzle flare.

'Anyone can hit the target with a thousand shots a minute,' Deino said over the inter-squad comm. He brought down his storm bolter and walked towards Lorenzo as other members of Squad Gideon converged from different directions. 'Your weapon lacks elegance.'

'Perhaps, my brother,' Leon replied. 'However, it would take forever to shoot all of them one at a time.'

Deino conceded the point without comment and turned around to cover the entranceway he'd just come through. Something moved across the beams of his suit lamps and Deino fired, the shot blowing an arm from the genestealer. The second round shattered its hip, ripping its leg from its body.

'If you can't enjoy the artistry of war, then what's the point of fighting?' Deino asked nobody in particular.

00.12.13

'Allow me,' said Gideon, appearing at Lorenzo's right, his shield arm extended.

Lorenzo grabbed the proffered limb and allowed himself to be helped to his feet. The two sergeants raised their fists in salute to each other.

Gideon's squad were showing signs of hard fighting. Each warrior's armour had scars of battle – cracked plates, gouged ceramite and exposed sublayer cables and pipes – rapidly repaired by the Techmarines back at the impact zone. Gideon's helm had an impressive rent across the mouth grille and the entire right side of Leon's armour was pitted with shards of metal and recently applied welding where his destroyed assault cannon had been replaced. All were stained by alien gore and a few had bloodstains from their own wounds.

Lorenzo realised his own squad's appearance was now less

than satisfactory. The joints in his armour's left arm were stiff and his helm actuators had broken when the genestealer had tried to twist off his head. He could only look straight ahead. Peeling paint sloughed from charred ceramite on Zael's armour, evidence of a desperate close-range shot from his heavy flamer. Valencio was missing most of his left shoulder pad and the emblem on his chestplate was scored with three ragged claw marks. Only Deino appeared unmarked; apparently no genestealer had yet avoided his cool marksmanship.

'Still intact,' said Valencio, holding up the C.A.T., which dejectedly waved its appendages.

'Good,' said Lorenzo. He switched the comms to the command frequency. 'Brother-captain, this is Lorenzo. The unit has been secured and is still functional.'

There was a hiss of static before Captain Raphael replied.

'The Angel's blessing upon you,' he said. 'We need the data of the deeper levels to devise the next phase. Without it I have no recourse but bombardment. Return the unit to the Techmarines in grid alpha and re-arm.'

'Acknowledged,' said Lorenzo. He turned to Gideon and activated the inter-squad frequency. 'Would you like to go front or back?'

'We'll lead the push back to the perimeter,' said Gideon. 'Watch our backs.'

'Affirmative,' said Lorenzo.

Lorenzo organised his warriors' dispositions as Gideon and his men headed off. The two squads plunged into the maze of corridors. Storm bolter fire and the deadly peal of Leon's assault cannon heralded their progress through the twist of metal and plascrete. More and more genestealers were arriving from their hibernation nest somewhere deep inside the hulk, and the sensorium swarmed with contact blips.

Metre by hard-fought metre Squads Gideon and Lorenzo battled through the aliens, reaping a bloody harvest of vengeance with their weapons. Gideon's hammer and Lorenzo's power sword blazed like beacons in the dark artificial caverns and long tunnels. The flare of muzzle flash and the ruddy glow of flames marked the Blood Angels' passing.

00.12.83

In the ruins of a derelict merchantman's hold, clothed in the darkness of the void, something stirred. It surfaced slowly from anabiosis, frozen limbs and organs gradually warming, alien synapses starting to spark.

All was still instinct and impressions, with no true intelligence yet. Its brood were rousing around it, their minds touching and connecting. Images flickered through its wakening subconscious. Large creatures of bright red impenetrable skin killed its progeny with fire and blade. Even as more of its offspring surfaced to consciousness and joined the brood mind, others disappeared.

One impulse rose above all others, an evolutionary imperative that obscured all other consideration. It spread from the creature, rippling out through the brood, instilling them with a single directive.

Destroy.

00.13.00

Within the cordon of the breach head, the noses of boarding torpedoes jutted from the punctured wall like the petals of gigantic metal flowers. Protected by a ring of Terminators fighting the genestealers only a few hundred metres distant, Techmarines and their serfs laboured constantly to keep the squads armed and battle-ready.

Lorenzo was being attended by Brother Auletio, one of

the Techmarines. The spider-like arms of Auletio's servo harness backpack worked deftly with saws, drills and welders, repairing the damage to the radiator vents on Lorenzo's back. Sparks cascaded to the oil-stained decking, falling amongst piles of bolts and coils of cable and other detritus of repair.

Valencio approached, a robed orderly fussing around him with a paint gun, respraying the Terminator's armour. He had removed his helmet – something Lorenzo had tried to do but failed – and his eyes were bright with pride.

'Our brothers are deciphering the C.A.T. data now,' Valencio said. 'They seem very pleased.'

'As well they should,' said Lorenzo. 'We need all the information we can gather if we are to be victorious.'

'Our brothers fight bravely and do the Chapter honour,' said Valencio. 'I hope that I have acquitted myself with equal glory.'

Lorenzo did not reply immediately, pondering whether to indulge Valencio's need for validation. He relented, remembering how eager he had been when he had joined the First Company. To be acknowledged as a veteran was a tribute that should not be taken lightly. And, in truth, Valencio deserved praise.

'You fought bravely and with skill.'

'My thanks for your words,' said Valencio with a deferential nod of the head. 'I wish only to serve the memories of those that came before us.'

Dark thoughts swirled into Lorenzo's mind, recollections of the nine hundred and fifty who had been lost. He pushed the memories back into the depths of his mind, suppressing them as he had done for six and a half centuries.

'We will rejoin the battle shortly,' the sergeant said. 'Make sure the others are ready.'

Valencio nodded and moved away, leaving Lorenzo to his thoughts.

'That is the best that I can do,' said Auletio, the servo-arms folding into place behind him. 'There's nothing I can do about the helm. It is jammed solid and I do not have the tools needed to release it.'

'Your efforts do you credit,' Lorenzo said reflexively. He had all but forgotten the Techmarine's presence. The sergeant lifted his arms while a pair of serfs attached chunky storm bolter magazines to his belt. 'Others are in more need of your attentions.'

'May the strength of the Angel fill your spirit,' said Auletio before turning away, his orderlies trailing after him like chicks after their mother.

A hand slapped down on Lorenzo's right shoulder and the sergeant turned to find Zael standing beside him. The rest of the squad were behind Zael, helmets locked in place, damage patched, weapons ready.

'It is time to admonish our foes once more,' said Zael.

'Yes, I feel the need to administer the justice of the Emperor,' growled Lorenzo. He drew his power sword and activated its glittering blade. 'Let us be the blade of the Angel's judgement!'

'Praise the Angel,' the others chorused, falling in behind Lorenzo as he stalked towards the front line.

Soon the clatter and chatter of the breach head was behind them. The echoing retorts of storm bolters and rebounding roars of assault cannons replaced the whirr of drills and crack of welders. In the mess of interlacing corridors, sub-vents, access ways and doors it was easier to navigate by the readings of the sensorium than by what could be seen or heard. Lorenzo identified the area his squad had been ordered to secure and signalled ahead to Sergeant Adion that they were approaching.

In turn, each of Lorenzo's squad replaced one of Adion's men, taking positions overlooking a wide causeway that had once been the main dorsal corridor of a ship. They did so in the midst of combat, taking up the relentless battle against the swarms of genestealers hurling themselves at the cordon.

'Keep an eye on the bulkheads to the right,' warned Adion as Lorenzo joined him. The sergeant loosed off a quick burst of fire at a genestealer clambering from a sub-duct before pointing to a wall some thirty metres away, heavily dented from the other side. 'They've tried to break through three times already and we used the flamer to burn them out. I can't say how much longer those bulkheads will hold.'

'Affirmative,' said Lorenzo, adding his own fire to that of Adion. Lorenzo checked that his warriors were in position and gave Adion a reassuring thump on the arm with the hilt of his sword. 'The area is secure, you can break off now. The Chapter shall honour your deeds.'

'The Angel stands watch,' Adion said in reply before backing away down the corridor, firing a parting salvo at the enemy.

00.14.52

Lorenzo divided his attention between firing his weapon, monitoring the enemy's movements on the sensorium and listening to the mission updates on the comm. The analysis of the C.A.T. data was complete and Captain Raphael had outlined the situation.

The genestealers, more than forty thousand of them, were in a dormant state, hidden in a cluster roughly one kilometre from the landing zone. The ship in which they had made their lair seemed relatively intact, sealed from the vacuum and with minimal life support functions still operating. The same systems that maintained a modicum of temperature and atmosphere for the genestealers to survive could also prove to be their death. It was the captain's intent to use the air circulation system to poison the aliens as they hibernated. More Techmarines had arrived from the strike cruiser with tanks of lethal gas. Small-scale tests were being conducted at another point on the perimeter to determine the concentration of toxin required to kill the genestealers.

'If they're dormant, why don't we go in and slaughter them before they wake up?' asked Zael. 'One big push could wipe them out. These delays give the enemy more time to rise and gather their numbers.'

'That's what we thought last time,' Lorenzo replied quietly. 'At first it was just as you say; we slaughtered hundreds of them. Our attack caused some change, a shift in their behaviour. Each one that fell seemed to trigger the waking of ten more. They responded quickly, thousands of them emerging from their stasis within seconds. They surrounded us in minutes.'

Lorenzo did not have to continue. All present knew the rest of the tale. A shameful day in the Blood Angels' otherwise glorious history.

'Today the debt from that black day will be repaid,' said Zael. 'We will destroy this loathsome foe and restore our pride.'

'The Angel wills it,' said Valencio. 'Praise Lord Sanguinius!'

They fought on without further word for some time, each Terminator concentrating his efforts on killing the enemy. Gunfire reverberated constantly along the hallway and the corpses piled upon the concourse now numbered several hundred.

Then, as if some unseen hand had closed a door or shut off a tap, the attacks suddenly stopped. The silence that descended was more unnerving than the riotous clamour of battle, and Lorenzo steadied himself with thoughts of his primarch and the Chapter.

'Synchronise your sensorium data with Omnio,' Gideon's

voice drifted over the comm. 'He has noticed something important.'

Lorenzo adjusted his sensorium to receive data over the inter-squad comm. This had the effect of increasing its range, at the expense of clarity. There were two patches of green fog – clusters of indistinct contacts. Both were growing: one a hundred and fifty metres ahead, the other some seventy metres to the right flank.

'There has been a pattern in the attacks,' Omnio explained. 'They have been working systematically along the perimeter, seeking weak points. I believe they were attacking to judge our firepower and numbers, learning from our tactics and responses.'

'And now?' asked Lorenzo.

'That sounds very sophisticated,' Deino said, doubt in his voice.

'My observations are accurate,' said Omnio. 'The next attack will be from two directions simultaneously at the point between our curtains of fire.'

Flashing red icons highlighted a route through the corridors that would cut between the two squads with the minimum of exposure to the guns of the Terminators. The second attack would encircle Gideon and his men.

'We have to close the gap,' said Gideon. 'We cannot allow them to break through.'

'That will leave you vulnerable on your right,' Lorenzo pointed out, studying the schematic.

'Yes,' said Gideon.

'Very well,' said Lorenzo. 'Deino and Zael, move to the right and close off that path. Valencio, take Deino's place on point.'

Gideon was reorganising his squad's dispositions as well. The attack came before they were fully in position. Dozens of genestealers raced forward, the smudges of green splitting into separate contacts on the sensorium as the range closed. Zael used his flamer to close off a side-tunnel. Deino joined his fire with that of Scipio from Gideon's squad, creating a crossfire in one of the rooms the genestealers now had to pass through. Zael moved forward with the cleansing fire of his weapon, like shutting a lid on a box.

Gideon's squad was hard-pressed on the right, the aliens coming within only a few metres before revealing themselves. The sergeant's icon was at the forefront of the battle and Lorenzo could imagine Gideon standing firm with storm shield and thunder hammer, protecting his men. Lorenzo fought the urge to move across and aid his battle-brother. The line had to be held. He whispered a benediction to the Angel on behalf of Gideon and his men, and turned his attention back to the dark corridor ahead.

00.13.88

The genestealer attack was in full force. Multiple swarms of the creatures came at the Terminators from different directions, splitting them, dividing their attentions. From the reports over the comm Gideon knew that Space Marine casualties were mounting.

'Defensive posture is weakening,' announced Captain Raphael. 'Techmarine analysis of toxin effect complete. Now we attack. All squads converge on primary hibernation site for final extermination. The scene of our reprisal is set. We are the avengers. Nemesis.'

'Finally,' growled Leon. He unleashed a furious burst of fire from his assault cannon, clearing a junction ahead and stomped forwards eagerly.

'Purge the xenos!' said Gideon, moving up behind Leon. 'Blood Angels, the time of our retribution is nigh.'

'Breach head infiltrated!' Captain Raphael warned over the command channel. 'Brothers Auletio and Cannavaro are compromised. Gideon and Lorenzo, fix on their beacon signals. Now transmitting their suit frequencies. Insufficient time for rescue. Establish viability of missing brethren. Destroy if necessary. Protect our gene-seed.'

'Affirmative,' said Gideon, feeling suddenly deflated. The signal came through on his sensorium – two red blips pulsed roughly three hundred metres away. 'Signal received. Moving out.'

'Prayers of vengeance steel our souls,' said Raphael and then he was gone.

'Lorenzo, take the signal at grid eighteen-kappa,' said Gideon. 'We shall deal with the signal at twenty-kappa.'

'Affirmative, moving alongside your advance,' replied Lorenzo.

Leon was at a cross-junction, firing to the left. Gideon moved behind him and took up a defensive stance to the right. As Scipio pressed on between them, a line of genestealers emerged up a ramp in front of the sergeant.

'Suffer the wrath of the Blood Angels!' he bellowed, stepping forward to meet their charge.

Swinging his hammer, he smashed aside the first of the genestealers, its shattered body crashing into the metal wall of the narrow corridor. A second alien leapt towards Gideon and he brought up his shield. Lightning arced along the creature's outstretched claws as it struck, sending the creature into a spasm. Gideon barely brought his shield around to ward away another genestealer attacking from his right. Shifting his bulky armour in the tight space, Gideon brought his hammer down onto the head of the stunned creature.

Another was on him in moments, slashing at his abdomen, its diamond-hard claws raking strips of metal and splinters of ceramite.

Gideon used the edge of his shield as a weapon, bringing it down onto the ridged nodules of chitin protecting the creature's neck. There was a snap and the genestealer wilted to the floor. A flurry of detonations ahead cut apart two more genestealers and Omnio came into view from a side passage, his storm bolter blazing.

'Flank secured,' Omnio announced, turning his weapon towards the ramp and unleashing another salvo.

Gideon slewed his armour one hundred and eighty degrees and marched back to the junction, before turning right and following Scipio's path. Leon advanced along a parallel course, the intermittent roar of his assault cannon echoing from ahead of Gideon. As usual, Noctis brought up the rear. Quiet and dependable, Noctis fired off bursts from his storm bolter at the genestealers circling behind the squad, retreating a few steps when the opportunity allowed. Gideon slowed his own progress, allowing Noctis to catch up. No one would be left isolated this time.

A yellow glare ahead announced the arrival of Brother Zael from Squad Lorenzo. Flames flickered along the tunnel, searing through a cluster of genestealers that had leapt from an overhead gantry to land behind Scipio. The aliens writhed in the flames for a second or two and then collapsed into smouldering heaps as the inferno dissipated. Patches of burning promethium scarred the walls and floor. Gideon ignored them and pushed through the dying fires to keep pace with Scipio who was now twenty metres ahead.

'Room, thirty metres to the right,' said Gideon. 'Noctis, cover the approach.'

'Understood,' replied Noctis as he peeled away from the main corridor.

00.14.62

The sensorium showed a steady stream of genestealers approaching the two squads from ahead and behind. Noctis raised a hand in greeting as he saw Zael pass a junction in front of him.

'They'll no sooner pass me than the Gates of Varl,' said Zael as he disappeared into the gloom.

Noctis said nothing. The corridor ahead was blocked by several doors, like airlocks. Blips of the sensorium showed that genestealers were lurking close by. Noctis opened fire on the closest door, blasting it into pieces. Three genestealers turned towards the Terminator, surprised. He fired calmly, gunning down all three in two short bursts. His heavy footfalls reverberating along the corridor, Noctis advanced resolutely, firing at the next door. Another genestealer was revealed by the door's demise and it suffered the same fate as the others, its blood spattering across a riveted bulkhead.

Two more doors later and Noctis finally reached the room to which he had been assigned. It was a loading bay of some kind, the mangled remnants of cranes and lifters angled madly in the shadows above. Huge blast doors had been burst inwards by the impact of another vessel at some immeasurably distant time in the past and an outcrop of a crenulated balcony punctured the doorway. Genestealers leapt over the parapet to the floor of the bay, landing sure-footedly and springing towards Noctis without hesitation.

Noctis fired dispassionately, regarding the aliens sprinting towards him as nothing more than moving targets. He paced his fire, unleashing rounds in sensible double-bursts so as not to jam the mechanism of the storm bolter. When he was down to his last few rounds, he turned his fire upon the balcony, gunning down the genestealers perched on the wall. Having given himself a couple of seconds' grace with this act, he ejected the empty magazine and slammed in another.

The Terminator locked the stabilising bars in the knees of his armour and settled into a solid firing posture. He began to hum quietly as he fired; the *Hymn of the Angel Resurgent*. He kept the beat with the crack of bolt rounds. He wasn't going anywhere for a while.

00.15.03

Some form of automatic response had sealed all of the doors in this part of the ship. Perhaps the hull had been breached and integrity had been lost, or maybe the ship had come under attack. Whatever the cause, the sealed doors were proving problematic. Line of sight was only a few metres in each direction and Lorenzo was forced to take the lead, his power sword a surer defence than his squad's power fists against the genestealer ambushes. Rents in his armour and caked gore bore testament to the fury of those encounters.

The pulsing icon of Brother Auletio's signal was a few metres ahead. It was surrounded by enemy contact signals. Lorenzo levelled his storm bolter at the door and fired, its rusting frame exploding under the fusillade. The rapid-fire buzz of Leon's assault cannon sounded somewhere to the right, close to Cannavaro's ident-signal.

Six genestealers poured from the room. The first was thrown back by Lorenzo's opening salvo, the alien behind deftly leaping over its tattered corpse. Lorenzo pulled the trigger to let loose another barrage of destruction but only a single bolt fired before his weapon jammed. The shell took the genestealer high in the chest, knocking it sideways. It staggered to its feet, fanged maw open.

'I am the blade of Sanguinius!' Lorenzo cried, charging forwards.

His power sword cleaved the head of the genestealer from its body. Another alien took its place, claws smashing into Lorenzo's left shoulder as it pounced. The sergeant thrust upwards, lancing his sword through the creature's exposed throat. The genestealer twisted as it fell, dragging Lorenzo's arm to one side, the power sword trapped between its vertebrae.

'Clear for fire!' shouted Deino. Lorenzo ripped free his sword and hurled himself backwards into a narrow side-corridor, smashing against the wall. Bolts screamed past where the sergeant had been a moment before and droplets of thick blood splattered the passageway.

'Move ahead and secure,' ordered Lorenzo as he righted himself.

Deino advanced past and Lorenzo fell in behind. Upon entering the room at the end of the passageway, Deino stopped suddenly.

'Emperor's mercy,' the normally cool Terminator muttered.

Lorenzo moved into the room, stepping past Deino. Scraps of red armour littered the chamber and a severed servo arm twitched in one corner, gouging a furrow into the tiles of the floor. Auletio sat with his back propped against the wall. His armour had been stripped away in many places and blood trickled from a gash across his face.

It was not the injuries to the Techmarine that had caused Deino such dismay; it was the rest of his appearance. Lorenzo could see that the Techmarine's flesh had a bluish tint to it. Auletio's skin was pocked with lesions and oddly shaped protuberances swelled underneath his pale skin. His veins were like thick cords across his arms and neck and his face was distorted. His eyes bulged and ridges were breaking through the skin of his brow. A lone fang punctured his upper lip, curving up towards his nose.

There was intelligence in Auletio's eyes, and terror. It was something Lorenzo had never seen in the eyes of another Space Marine. Auletio weakly raised an arm and groaned. Yellowish ichor oozed from his wounds, mixed with his thick blood.

'Target one located,' Lorenzo broadcast. 'Viability negative.'

'Same here,' replied Gideon from the location of the other downed Techmarine, his voice choked, his usual attention to comm protocol forgotten.

'Aggressive genetic mutation,' Omnio told them. His voice was measured and quiet. 'The genestealer's usual breeding function is to use an ovipositor to implant its seed within a victim, and this is passed on to the implantee's progeny. Space Marines do not follow the normal reproductive cycle. I would theorise that the implanted genetic material is reacting unpredictably with the Adeptus Astartes modifications. Projection: damage is permanent and irreversible. Suggest immediate destruction to avoid danger of contamination.'

'Zael, I need you up here, now!' Lorenzo bellowed, his anger fuelled by distaste. Genestealers were still attacking from several directions and Lorenzo forced himself to focus on the mission. 'Valencio, stand guard at rear station. Deino, push through and link up with Gideon.'

'Affirmative,' replied Deino, moving out of the room through another doorway.

'I shall protect,' said Valencio. The thump of his footfalls receded into the corridors.

'En route,' Zael announced.

Lorenzo turned his eyes away from Auletio's and span on the spot to stand over watch on the corridor Zael would be using. It made no difference; the Techmarine's plaintive stare still hovered in the sergeant's mind. Lorenzo remembered that his gun was still jammed and worked to clear the mechanism, dragging his thoughts back to the ongoing combat. A pair of genestealers appeared at the far end of the corridor as Lorenzo ejected the storm bolter's magazine. The sergeant smacked home a fresh clip of shells and opened fire, glad of the release.

It had been shame of the Blood Angels' past defeat that had driven on Lorenzo. Now a cold hatred filled him, far sharper and more motivating than any feeling of historical guilt. More genestealers boiled up from the deck below. Lorenzo fired long bursts from his storm bolter as the aliens converged on the room, the anger welling up inside him, threatening to break through. Lorenzo resisted the urge to charge forwards and administer revenge with his power sword, though every cell of his body screamed at him to let go of his discipline and indulge the bloodthirst that lurked beneath the skin of every Blood Angel.

A wave of incinerating fury from behind the knot of genestealers announced Zael's arrival and Lorenzo barely managed to check his fire. The sergeant stepped out of the room and into the side passage in which he had sheltered before, allowing Zael to pass.

'Cleanse and burn,' Lorenzo said, not looking back into the room, not wishing to see its awful contents again. He stood guard behind Zael as the Terminator reached the door.

'Cleanse and burn!' roared Zael and his flamer poured purifying fire into the chamber, reducing Auletio's remains to a charred heap within seconds. 'Go to the Angel and be proud of your sacrifice, Brother Auletio. You will be received with glory and forgiveness.'

The drawn-out rattle of an assault cannon from the other side of the deck followed shortly after.

'Objective terminated,' Gideon grimly announced on the comm.

'Objective terminated,' replied Lorenzo, his voice quivering with rage. 'Now, let us join the attack.'

00.15.55

At the heart of the space hulk, the creature that had newly surfaced to sentience flexed sinews and muscles that had been immobile for centuries. As strength returned to its body, so too did the numbers of the brood swell. More and more of its progeny awoke, spurred into consciousness by the imperative of the brood mind. It felt their presence and opened its eyes, recognising itself for the first time, understanding its purpose: broodlord. In the gloom, thousands of eyes glittered in the light from the false stars far above. The prey had been goaded into action and came closer. Hundreds of the brood perished as the red-skinned hunters advanced. It did not matter. They existed to die for the life of their brood.

Not in this place would it lurk. The others of its kind needed space to awaken; its brood-presence suppressed their stirring minds. Unfolding powerful limbs, stretching thawing sinews, the broodlord raised itself to its feet, towering above its progeny. Old recollections of dens and lairs, tunnels and pathways flickered into its memory. These were its hunting grounds, it knew their tangled web in every detail. Still stiff from its anabiosis, the creature stalked slowly across the chamber, its brood parting before it. Craning its neck to loosen tight fibres, extending joints long frozen by stasis, it compelled the brood to follow. It ducked into a hole rent into the

*wall and dropped to the ground below, its claws ringing on the
metal deck. Ahead lay the warren of tunnels where it would strike.
In the dark, the brood would wait. Their time was coming soon.*

00.18.29

There was little chatter between the members of Squads Lorenzo and Gideon, the veteran warriors disturbed by what had become of the captured Techmarines. Only the occasional muttered devotional broke the comm silence as the two sergeants led their men back through the space hulk towards the main Blood Angels force.

'Lorenzo and Gideon, this is Raphael,' the captain's voice broke through the quiet. 'We are locating suitable target points for release of toxins. Expecting high resistance. We have to thin the numbers of the enemy. You have a new mission. I need you to perform a diversionary attack. There is a secondary cluster of inactive life signals near to your position, at grid four-theta. Destroy the dormant genestealers and trigger a counter-attack from the main group.'

'Affirmative,' said Lorenzo, and Gideon gave a similar acknowledgement.

'Our moment of retribution approaches,' said Raphael.

'In the Angel's eyes we shall know victory,' replied Gideon.

The objective was clear on the sensorium – a mass of low-grade signals roughly two hundred metres away. Lorenzo detailed the squad into an attack formation and took a position in the middle of the group, ready to move forward to bolster the attack or fall back to defend the rear.

'Zael, your heavy flamer will be best suited to the annihilation of the incubating genestealers,' said Lorenzo. 'Conserve as much ammunition as possible en route.'

'Same for you, Leon,' said Gideon. 'Don't get carried away.'

There were grunts of disappointed consent from both Space Marines.

'What about this counter-attack?' asked Omnio. 'Direction? Strength?'

'Strength unknown, but I've been studying the schematic,' said Scipio. 'There's a long concourse that runs the length of the freight wreck where the main concentration in located. It comes up through what seems to be a series of collapsed elevator shafts. If we can gain the advantage of position we should be able to cut them down as they emerge.'

'Good,' said Lorenzo. 'We don't have time to destroy the dormants and then get to the defensive position. We'll set up a perimeter while you annihilate the target.'

'Understood,' said Gideon. 'We'll reinforce as soon as the mission is completed. Let the Emperor spread our hatred of the foe.'

'In his name we smite the unclean,' replied Lorenzo.

The two squads took diverging courses through the bowels of an old warship's gun batteries. Some distant reactor still trickled out a fitful stream of energy and red lights flickered overhead. Great arched windows of reinforced ferroglass were smashed and distorted, revealing a ruddy view of the tortured innards of another vessel.

While Gideon and his warriors cut into the depths of the frigate's interior, Lorenzo led his squad to the left through immense shadows cast by misshapen, corroded guns. The war engines of an age gone past were encased in crumbling bunkers of masonry, rusted supports jutting from the cracked and flaking rockcrete. Magazines where shells the size of tanks had once been stored were now chambers filled with dunes of oxidised metal and inert grey propellant. The Terminators waded thigh-deep through these artificial drifts, alert for danger, their attention never wavering from the telltale displays of the sensorium.

Perhaps stirred into life by the nearing presence of the Terminators, a few of the life forms on the scanner surged in activity. Their signals brightened and began to move. They did not come straight at the Space Marines, as they had done in the first minutes of the battle. They coalesced into small groups and then the groups drifted together, gathering their strength.

'Why don't they attack?' asked Valencio.

'Would you?' replied Deino.

Valencio thought about this for a moment.

'No,' he conceded. 'But I'm not an animal. I have reason and experience that tells me that attacking piecemeal is doomed to failure. These things have just woken, they cannot know what we are.'

'They learn, right enough,' growled Lorenzo. He shouldered open a door, the old metal screeching and disintegrating under the weight of his armour. Beyond lay a black corridor with doorless archways every few metres. 'Those that survived learnt from the deaths of the others. They changed and adapted quickly. Quicker than we could…'

'Psychic?' said Valencio.

'Very likely,' Lorenzo said, pausing beside the nearest arch and turning his suit to direct its lamps into the darkness. The cones of light revealed seized gears and broken chains with links larger than the Space Marines. The ceiling was lost in shadows, the ancient mechanism concealed hundreds of metres above. Lorenzo turned back to the main corridor. 'It does not matter how they do it. We must be ready, whatever their tactics.'

'Victory is the reward of the vigilant,' said Zael.

Footfalls muffled, their lights swallowed by the vastness of the gallery, the squad moved on towards the elevator shafts.

* * *

00.19.14

'Just like tar–' began Leon, but Scipio cut across him.

'Don't say it!' he hissed. 'You said that about the orks and I lost a leg. Look, there's movement on the sensorium.'

'Weapons check,' ordered Gideon, pressing the stud of his thunder hammer. Its heavy head glowed from within, sheathing the weapon with a blue aura. A test of his storm shield's power supply had equal success. Around him, the squad calibrated targeter links and checked magazines. Leon brought the rotating barrels of his assault cannon up to full speed and loosed off a short burst of fire at a pile of leaking barrels at the far end of the passageway. They disintegrated into metal splinters and puddles of thick fluid.

'Combat ready,' Leon reported, echoed by the other squad members.

The genestealers' nest was barely twenty metres away, across a narrow aqueduct-like bridge, with raised sides and a channel along its length through which trickled a thick green slime. The sensorium showed a concentration of more than thirty of the creatures just ahead, in a condensed mass of crushed rooms and contorted corridors.

'Quick, across the bridge,' said Gideon, waving Scipio forward. It was a sturdy structure, its plascrete piles covered with strange black moss but showing no damage. The gap below was shrouded in darkness and sensorium readings showed the drop to be approximately fifteen metres. Suspension cables creaked and groaned as the squad moved on to the bridge.

'There's something wrong with my sensorium link,' said Omnio. 'Brother-sergeant, I'm getting false readings.'

'Mine also,' said Leon.

Gideon checked his own sensorium and saw registered

life forms barely ten metres away. That would put them on the bridge.

'Overhead!' shouted Scipio, turning and firing above the heads of the squad. A four-armed body plummeted from the shadows of the bridge's suspension towers, trailing blood. Gideon looked up as best as his armour would allow and saw more shapes crawling across the ceiling and dropping onto the support pillars.

'Spread out, cover each other!' he shouted, raising his storm shield as a genestealer leapt the gap from pylon to bridge, landing a metre in front of the sergeant.

He smashed the creature from the aqueduct with a back-handed swipe of his hammer just as another genestealer landed behind him. Armour feedback warnings flashed red in his display as it gouged a long furrow though the back of his left leg. Turning awkwardly, he desperately fended off its next attack with his shield. All around, more aliens were dropping onto the bridge. The Terminators struggled to raise their weapons to the required elevation and were forced to resort to shooting their foes at hand-to-hand range and blasting the genestealers from each other's backs.

More genestealers swarmed along the bridge, cornering the squad from the front, left and right. Scipio smashed a creature to a pulp with a single blow from his power fist. Leon was cursing constantly, unable to use his assault cannon at such close quarters. An ammunition pack on Omnio's belt exploded, hurling a genestealer out into the void with a blossom of flame, Omnio lurching in the opposite direction. He stumbled against the retaining wall, the impact of his heavy suit crumbling the ancient plascrete.

As he righted himself, a genestealer landed on his shoulders and the wall turned to dust under their weight, sending the two of them sprawling into the shadows. Omnio's lamps span crazily in the darkness, tumbling for a moment and then going dark.

'Omnio!' Gideon bellowed, shoulder charging a gene-stealer, his momentum lifting the alien off its feet and throwing it over the edge of the bridge.

'Suit compromised, occupant intact,' Omnio replied, his voice calm and clear. 'Fell on some wreckage. Lamps damaged. System support integrity at eighty per cent. Power couplings intermittent to left arm and sensorium. Something has punctured my lower back. Injury not critical. Enemy… er… squashed.'

The sensorium was showing blips all around the squad, so close Gideon could not tell if they were above, below or right in front of him. Scipio had pushed through to the other end of the bridge and was standing overwatch. There were a few more genestealers still on the bridge, wreaking havoc.

'Can you see if there's anything else down there with you?' Gideon asked. He moved forwards, sweeping aside a genestealer clinging onto Noctis's storm bolter arm. Noctis gave a nod of thanks and took up position back-to-back with Scipio. His disciplined fire strafed across the bridge supports, the bodies of more genestealers tumbling into the darkness amidst the bolt detonations.

Crunches of powdering plascrete and groans of grinding metal echoed from below as Omnio pushed himself to his feet. A fitful light announced his location, intermittently strobing across the tangle of fallen pylons and cables from another bridge that had once run alongside the aqueduct.

'Nothing on infrared,' Omnio reported. 'Power unstable. Hard to walk. Going comm-silent to reroute power to sensorium. I'll meet you at the nest.'

'Affirmative, Omnio,' replied Gideon. He glanced around

and saw that the bridge was now clear of enemies. 'The Angel watches you in the darkness.'

'You too,' said Omnio and then his link turned to static.

The constant fire from Scipio demonstrated that more and more genestealers were awakening. However, the attack was having an effect. Captain Raphael spoke on the comm.

'Genestealer force breaking away from main concentration,' he announced. 'Good work, Gideon. Lorenzo, prepare for engagement. Estimate two thousand hostiles. No friendly forces in your area. Purge with freedom!'

'Affirmative,' said Lorenzo. 'Our vengeance shall be written in the blood of the foe.' There was a hiss as Lorenzo changed channel to inter-squad frequency. 'Gideon, request termination of target with utmost haste.'

'Affirmative,' said Gideon. 'We'll be as quick as we can. Hold on and watch our backs.'

'We will not fail,' Lorenzo assured his battle-brothers.

00.20.99

Its progeny fought and died. Under its urging they had amassed their numbers. Now they attacked in force, seeking to overwhelm the armoured hunters. Fire and explosions filled the metal hole the brood were using to approach their prey. Many fell, but more were coming. The brood mind pulsed and grew and the creature could feel its powers reaching their zenith.

It sensed the minds of the hunters, beyond the throbbing instinct of the brood, their spirits armoured, like their bodies. Meaningless chatter filled their thoughts, but through the core of their beings blazed a harsh light, encasing their souls and protecting them. It probed harder, seeking a weakness. Their anger and their hatred were powerful, concepts it knew of only from others of their kind who had come before. Concepts like fear and horror. The prey that had come before had been weak. These were strong. It would need to look upon them to break their barriers.

Gathering a bodyguard of genestealers about itself, the broodlord began to ascend the shaft, clawing its way up the metal walls. More fire engulfed those ahead, their burning corpses dropping past into the depths. It climbed swiftly, urging on the brood to swarm forwards.

It laid its eyes upon the first of them, the fire breather. The prey paused for a moment, the reflective lenses of its eyes fixing on the broodlord. The moment of hesitation was all the broodlord needed to extend the will of the broodmind and touch upon the mind of its victim. The hunter fought for a moment, struggling against the alien will invading its thoughts. Rather than succumb to the psychic suggestion, its brain shut out all thought and the armoured creature fell into a coma, collapsing heavily to the ground. The broodlord considered this impassively. The creatures would not be controlled, but they could be rendered vulnerable.

As more of the flaming projectile grubs bit at its flesh, the broodlord turned its gaze upon the next victim.

00.21.64

Leon's assault cannon tore apart the dormant genestealers, ripping through their hunched forms in a storm of shells and gore. In long lines they lay upon the floor of a high, arched chamber, like grotesque, giant foetuses. Many were covered with patches of lichen and the webs of spiders. Clusters of insect eggs mottled their chitinous hide and whole streams of slick plant life trailed from crouched bodies. Some of the genestealers woke amidst the tumult but were quickly cut down. It was butchery, and it filled Gideon with righteous warmth as he watched the destruction of his enemies.

'There's more down here,' said Scipio, pointing towards the shadows underneath the splitting remains of some gigantic pulpit.

'Enjoy yourself,' said Leon, turning the assault cannon onto another row of hibernating aliens. 'I'm busy.'

'Thank you,' said Scipio, opening fire with his storm bolter. Screeches of pain echoed along the cathedral, stopped abruptly as Scipio continued to fire.

'Squad Gideon, this is Laertes,' a voice came through on the comm, another Terminator sergeant. 'Verify position of Squad Lorenzo. They're supposed to be guarding our flank.'

'They are just to your...' began Gideon, checking the sensorium and wondering why Laertes even needed to ask. He stopped because something was wrong. The life signals of Lorenzo and his squad were clear enough, but they were unmoving. Swarms of contacts were moving past their location. 'I cannot confirm their status. Can you investigate? Objective almost complete, we will join you shortly.'

'Affirmative, Gideon,' said Laertes. 'Remain on mission.'

'Bring light to the places of shadow,' said Gideon.

'We bear the Angel's flaming torch,' Laertes replied.

00.22.37

During more than three centuries of war, Claudio had never encountered such reckless ferocity. Orks were savage and ill-disciplined, but their will could be broken. The cold frenzy and utter disregard of the genestealers meant that no matter how many he slew, they kept attacking. It was alien and unnerving, and that meant Claudio fought all the harder.

He slashed and swiped with his suit's lightning claws, each fist armed with several blades as long as swords wreathed in arcing energy. Electricity spat and crackled as he carved open the ribcage of a genestealer, its blood hissing into vapour. Claws met claws as another alien attacked. The Terminator's weapons sheared through its arms and he decapitated the genestealer with a purposeful flick of the wrist.

'Sergeant!' he called out, but there was no response. 'Angelo? Germanus? Victis?'

A glance at the sensorium confirmed that the rest of the squad were dead. A wave of wrath flowed through Claudio at the realisation, matched by the surge of power through his armour as he broke into a lumbering run, striking out to the left and right as he ploughed through the genestealers massed around him.

'The Angel demands justice!' he roared, gouging the entrails from an alien to his right. He cut through the spine of another and cleaved the leg from a third. 'Death demands vengeance!'

For all his anger, Claudio was surrounded. Alien claws scratched at his shoulder pads and raked across his chestplate. Leering fanged faces appeared out of the darkness, teeth clamped onto his arms and legs. He felt their blows punching through his armour, digging into flesh and bone. Pain suppressants and healing stimulants flowed through his suit, stemming the blood flow and washing away the agony. With a wordless shriek, Claudio threw back his attackers, lightning claws glittering.

Blue lightning spat from the darkness, leaping from one genestealer to the next. Heads exploded and eyeballs steamed as the bolt continued its haphazard course. Within moments the corridor was empty of foes. Only their smoking corpses remained. A massive figure stepped into the lamplight, his armour painted blue in the heraldry of the Librarium.

'Brother Calistarius!' gasped Claudio.

The figure turned his helmed head towards Claudio, as if noticing him for the first time. Motes of sparkling energy played around the sword in his hand and danced along the cables entwining the Librarian's helm.

'Brother Claudio,' he replied in quiet recognition. 'It is good that you are alive.'

Claudio was not so sure. His battle-brothers had all been slain. He decided to change the subject.

'What of Squad Lorenzo?'

'They are alive,' Calistarius replied. 'For the moment. Come with me, we must hasten to their rescue.'

'Rescue?' asked Claudio as he fell in behind the Librarian.

'An alien psychic attack has paralysed their nervous systems. They live but are immobile. I feel their desperation. The enemy will return and kill them if we do not reach them first.'

'Squad Gideon is closer, you must warn them!'

'I have already apprised Gideon of the situation,' Calistarius said patiently. 'They are still completing the annihilation mission. We will rendezvous with Gideon once I have revived Lorenzo and his squad.'

They ducked in turn beneath the crooked lintel of a doorway, passing into a series of rooms with ceilings that bowed down as if a great weight were pressing on them. Ahead, the sensorium glowed with contact echoes.

'It is just the two of us?' asked Claudio.

'You were giving good account of yourself before I arrived,' said Calistarius 'I can feel your determination like a furnace in my mind.'

Claudio was uncomfortable with the idea of the Librarian sensing his thoughts, and then caught himself, wondering if these doubts were equally transparent. Claudio decided to occupy himself with another matter.

'This psychic attack, I do not understand why we have not encountered it before,' he said.

'Something has changed,' the Librarian replied. 'There is a guiding force, a focus that I can sense. Something new, yet something... *old*.'

There was something about the way Calistarius said the word that lurked in the recesses of Claudio's mind. Space Marines could know no fear, but the Terminator had a feeling of foreboding, of an emerging threat not yet fully comprehended. It was an unpleasant sensation and he tried to dismiss it.

'I will need you to protect me while I revive the others,' warned Calistarius. 'I must enter their minds and rouse them from their paralysis. I must be in close proximity to each one of them and my attention will be momentarily elsewhere.'

'My claws will be your shield,' Claudio promised.

Ascending an open, winding staircase of rusted metal, the Terminators came upon a dense huddle of rooms. The gene-stealers were returning, coming from the right, while the markers of Lorenzo and his squad were to the left.

'Let us be swift and bolster our numbers,' said Calistarius, turning to the left.

The Librarian stopped immediately and Claudio almost walked into his back. Ahead a heavy pressure door had dropped almost to the floor. There was enough of a gap that it seemed open on the sensorium, but in truth the warriors' bulky Terminator armour was not capable of stooping low enough to pass.

'Make way,' said Claudio. Calistarius backed up, allowing his comrade to stand before the door. Diverting as much reserve power as he could find to his lightning claws, Claudio launched himself at the pressure door. Electricity crawled across its surface as he plunged his blades into the barrier. His suit protesting with groans and whines, Claudio carved an opening, metal falling to the floor in molten droplets, sparks bouncing from his armour. With a punch, he sent a door-sized portion of the bulkhead tumbling and clanging along the corridor beyond.

'Hurry,' Claudio said, ducking through the opening.

The Librarian was close on his heels and the two of them stomped towards the closest flashing icon. Deino lay slumped in the corner of a small chamber that must once have served as some form of medical facility. Dulled scalpels, oxide-stained drills and other instruments sat in neat rows on rusted workbenches, undisturbed for millennia. An overturned gurney scored with claw marks lay to one side. Deino was unmoving but his life signal was slow and steady. His storm bolter was still held tightly in his grip.

'Rouse him,' urged Claudio. Calistarius said nothing as he crossed the room. He sheathed his sword and a nimbus of blue energy swathed his empty hand. The Librarian laid it upon the brow of Deino's helm and the light flowed over the unconscious Space Marine. Seconds passed and Claudio fretted, watching the closing sensorium signals.

With a wheeze of mechanical joints, Deino sat up. He raised his storm bolter and looked around.

'Eyes…' he muttered. Calistarius helped him to stand. 'Where are the others?'

'Near at hand, and alive,' Calistarius told him. The Librarian turned towards Claudio. 'It was a psychic attack, but our battle-brothers' sleep is natural. They can be woken normally. We should split up and restore the others.'

'I will attend to the sergeant,' said Claudio.

Deino nodded and turned towards the door. 'I shall find Brother Zael.'

'Sergeant Gideon approaches,' said Calistarius. 'We need to

link up with his squad as soon as possible. When Brother Zael is awake, send him to Gideon.'

While Calistarius stepped into the ward next door, Deino advanced into the corridors on the far side of the medical bay. Claudio headed out the door by which he had entered. He steered himself towards the signal from Lorenzo's suit, barely fifteen metres away. Looking at his sensorium, the Terminator knew that the first of the genestealers would be upon him before he reached the sergeant. Lightning claws crackling, he stalked along the passageway.

The closest sensorium blip resolved itself into three life forms and within a heartbeat they raced along the corridor towards Claudio. More were moving, out of sight, towards Deino and the Librarian. Claudio stopped and took up a fighting stance, legs braced, lightning claws raised.

'I am vengeance,' he snarled as the first genestealer leapt at him. With a blast of energy, the Terminator's lightning claws sheared the creature in half, flinging the ragged remains against the walls. Claudio punched the blades of his right fist through the chest of the second alien and carved the head from the third. As Claudio advanced the remains of the genestealer slid from his claws, leaving a bloody trail behind him.

More genestealers intercepted Claudio before he reached Lorenzo. The Blood Angel seethed with fury as he hacked and slashed his way forward. Images of his battle-brothers burned in his mind: Sergeant Leodinus welcoming Claudio to the squad; sparring with Angelo at the fortress-monastery; Germanus winning the Swordsman's Laurel Victis; using his chainfist to cut through the hull of a traitor tank. Last and most painful was the memory of Caladonis. They had joined the Scout Company at the same time, fought side-by-side in the Sixth Company and eventually became Terminators together. Truly they had been battle-brothers.

Even as the rage threatened to overwhelm Claudio he found himself at the door to the chamber where Lorenzo had fallen. Panting, he sliced the arm from a genestealer and cut open its throat. Claudio's suit was making all manner of warning noises about his pulse rate and blood pressure, threatening even the superhuman system of a Space Marine. Composing his rampaging thoughts, he turned into the room.

Sergeant Lorenzo lay draped over a pile of genestealer bodies, his power sword jutting from the spine of a dead foe. Checking there were no genestealers close at hand, Claudio deactivated his claws, the simple act calming him further. He laid a hand reverentially on Lorenzo's shoulder and shook him. There was no response.

'Sergeant?' Claudio barked across the inter-squad, grabbing Lorenzo with both hands and rolling him to his back.

In a heartbeat Lorenzo was up, shoving Claudio back. The sergeant swept up his sword, its blade stopping just short of Claudio's head. Claudio grabbed Lorenzo's wrist and pushed it to one side.

'I'm sorry,' said Lorenzo, stepping back, obviously disoriented. 'I thought you were the creature. What happened?'

'Explanations and apologies can wait, brother-sergeant,' Claudio said, stooping to retrieve Lorenzo's storm bolter from where it had been dropped to the decking. He handed the weapon to the sergeant and faced the door. With a thrum of power and a burst of electricity, Claudio activated his claws once more. 'The enemy await their punishment.'

The two of them headed back towards the others, Lorenzo providing covering fire for Claudio as he chopped his way through the warren of tunnels and rooms. Zael reported over the comm that he was awake and was moving with Calistarius to link up with Gideon's squad. Deino had roused Valencio to consciousness and the pair were fighting back-to-back against increasing numbers of genestealers. Goriel had recovered also and was trying his best to fight his way through to his sergeant.

00.25.08

Their forces scattered by the enemy's psychic attack, it took several minutes for the Terminators to join each other. As Lorenzo and Claudio met with Goriel, Calistarius arrived with Gideon close behind. Zael had been despatched to protect their rear.

As Gideon's squad filed past, Lorenzo counted only four warriors. He realised that Brother Omnio was missing.

'We shall grieve for the fallen even as we avenge them,' said Lorenzo as Gideon stopped beside him.

'He fell into the darkness,' Gideon replied, anger in his voice. 'No brother should die alone.'

'A means for our revenge may be close by,' Calistarius cut in. 'When I reached into the mind of Brother Deino, I detected the lingering presence of something else, and I felt it also when I woke Brother Goriel.'

Gunfire from further down the corridor heralded the arrival of Deino and Valencio. Their suits of armour were much scarred and bloodied, but both appeared to be free from serious injury.

'I'm glad somebody realises there's still fighting to be done,' said Scipio.

'Yes, we should join the attack on the main enemy cluster,' said Gideon. 'Every warrior will be needed.'

'Wait!' said Calistarius as Lorenzo turned away. 'You have not yet heard what I have to say.'

'My apologies, Brother-Librarian,' said Lorenzo, turning

back to face Calistarius. 'Deino, Valencio, Goriel, set up a perimeter.'

'Join them, Scipio, as you are so eager to fight,' said Gideon. There was a grunt of disappointment from Brother Leon. 'I have not forgotten you, Leon. Relieve Brother Zael as rear guard.'

'Acknowledged,' growled Leon and he set off at speed.

'What wisdom do you bring, Brother Calistarius?' Leon asked the Librarian. Storm bolter fire sounded along the corridors. 'I ask only that you be brief in your explanation.'

'Can you not sense its presence?' said the Librarian. 'Can you not feel a singing in your blood? There is some *thing* close at hand that calls to us. The Angel is guiding our feet upon a different path.'

Lorenzo remained silent. He was aware of a strange sensation within. It was almost below awareness, a tiny nagging feeling in his mind. It felt as if a distant chorus was singing a war-hymn at the edge of hearing and its dimly heard refrain stirred his blood. The sergeant felt a little more energised than he had done before. The retorts of the storm bolters sounded sharper. The flash of muzzle flares appeared a little brighter. He felt more *alive*.

'I feel it,' the sergeant said. 'What is it?'

'I do not know,' Calistarius admitted. 'But I can find it.'

'I feel it also,' said Gideon. 'Could this not be some trick of the enemy? We should join the others.'

'It is the Angel's siren song,' said Calistarius, his words quiet, almost ethereal. 'There is no taint, no impurity in that holy voice.' The Librarian pointed over Lorenzo's shoulder, towards Deino and the others. His voice was firm once more. 'It is this way.'

'We cannot be distracted from our primary mission,' said Gideon. 'The attack on the alien nest is our objective. Those are Captain Raphael's orders.'

'Go to your brothers,' said Calistarius with no hint of annoyance. 'With the captain's permission, I shall seek this object myself.'

'My squad will escort you,' said Lorenzo. 'You are too valuable to lose in this manner, Brother-Librarian. I cannot allow you to go alone.'

There was a moment of silence and Lorenzo detected the buzz of a secure transmission close at hand.

'I have informed Captain Raphael of our plan and he gives us his blessing,' said Calistarius. 'We will see you again soon enough, Sergeant Gideon.'

'Very well, I agree,' said Gideon, though it was plain from his tone that he did not like the idea. 'We shall return to the main force and Lorenzo shall follow our revered Brother-Librarian. Do not spend too long on this.'

'May the Angel will it,' said Lorenzo.

00.26.11

They encountered only scattered groups of genestealers as Calistarius guided Squad Lorenzo through the twisting depths towards the source of the phenomenon; most of the aliens were concentrating their attacks on the main Blood Angels force. Now and then a burst of storm bolter fire or the crackle of the Librarian's psychic powers echoed back down the corridors to Goriel, who was stationed at the rear of the makeshift squad. There was no threat to the rear and Goriel felt a growing frustration at his inaction.

Ever since he had been roused from the psychic attack, Goriel had felt different. More whole. He could feel the emanating sensation that Calistarius had described. It was something that lingered in his mind and pulsed through his veins with every beat of his hearts. Something in the darkness was reaching out to him and his entire being was reaching back.

They passed into a wide, open deck, with a high vaulted ceiling and a long gallery of tall arched windows. An immense shape blotted out the view of the stars, the bulk of a ship crushed into the side of the vessel they were currently investigating. The floor and ceiling of the chamber were buckled and the Terminators had to clamber over folded ridges of metal. In the wide space they spread into a line abreast and Goriel made his way over to the left flank, close to the windows.

The further they advanced, the more Goriel felt the tug of the presence Brother Calistarius had detected. It seemed that each step filled Goriel with greater energy, that every stride brought him closer to some goal that he had longed for but never known. He swivelled to the left and right, suit lamps dancing over the haphazardly corrugated deck as he searched for enemies. He stopped and turned fully to his left, allowing the lights to penetrate the darkness beyond the windows. What they revealed caused him to gasp in amazement.

'Sergeant,' he croaked, his wonder choking the words in his throat.

'What is it?' answered Lorenzo.

'Look,' Goriel whispered back.

In the twin glares of his lamps the side of the neighbouring vessel was revealed. It was large and had settled against the hulk at a steep angle. The view from the window was restricted, but despite its unfamiliar tilt and partial obscurity, the blazon upon the side of the vessel was instantly recognisable: the winged blood drop of the Blood Angels.

'By the grace of the Angel,' said Lorenzo, hushed. The others looked on in dumbfounded silence.

'We have been brought here for a purpose,' Calistarius eventually said. 'We all hear the call and must answer it.'

'We have to find a way to gain entry,' said Goriel, turning so that his lamps played over the walls of the large chamber. A tangle of wreckage sprawled from floor to ceiling where the two vessels had collided, creating a jarring vista of warped decks and contorted bulkheads.

'We will find a way in,' said Lorenzo.

The sergeant led the squad as quickly as the undulating floor would allow, until the Terminators were standing before the wall of twisted metal and broken rockcrete. They split up along the length of the barrier, seeking a way to climb up or break through. Zael pulled at girders with his power fist and answering creaks from above warned that the mass was unstable. Goriel spied a half-hidden airlock portal about five metres above his head. His excitement growing, he sought some means of ascending to its level.

'Careful,' said Lorenzo. 'Check the sensorium.'

There were life signals beyond the mass of metal, inside the Blood Angels ship. The thought of genestealers aboard provoked two responses in Goriel. The first was hope, for if they had found a way to gain entry, so too would the Terminators. The second was anger, and his desire to get aboard and cleanse the taint of the alien from the sacred decks of the ancient ship fuelled his search.

'Over here!' Valencio called out. He was bent to one knee, his lamps shining into a dark hole that came up to waist height. 'I think there's a pressure door here, if we can get to it.'

Valencio's chainfist spat sparks as he cut through metal struts. Goriel and Zael added the strength of their power fists, pulverising blocks of ferrocrete and bending girders out of Valencio's path. It did not take long to clear access to the exterior doorway.

'Make way,' said Calistarius and the others stepped back to allow him to reach the door. The Librarian examined the portal, running a gauntleted hand over the seals, his eyes lingering for a while on a keypad set into a recess next to the door. 'We will have to force it.'

Clearing more space for themselves to work, the Terminators unearthed two huge hinges. Valencio set to cutting through the immense bolts while the others used their power fists to batter handholds into the thick steel. A minute's labour was rewarded when, with a shriek of tearing metal, the door sagged inwards and then crashed to the ground. Goriel was the first through, shoving aside the wreckage. He found himself in an access hatch that opened out onto a long corridor that ran a considerable length of the ship in each direction.

'Contact!' he yelled, opening fire as a genestealer scuttled around a corner and bounded towards him.

The others followed swiftly through the airlock and took up defensive positions as more genestealers spilled into the corridor. Seeing their bodies torn apart by the explosive bolts of the Terminators filled Goriel with a growing elation. More than ever before, the deaths of his foes sang in his veins. Each death was a blow struck in vengeance; vengeance for the massacre six hundred years past. Yet it was something more than that. The resonance that throbbed through his being had grown stronger the closer he had come to the ancient Blood Angels vessel. Thoughts not entirely of his own creation flittered through his mind: glimpses of worlds and foes he had never seen. Fighting back the images trying to crowd into his mind, Goriel gunned down the genestealers with joy.

The first wave of genestealer attacks was halted, though others were near at hand and closing fast. Lorenzo ordered the squad to move towards the prow of the vessel, seeking some clue as to its identity. The sergeant sent Goriel ahead as he stopped at a dust-carpeted display panel and grid of runekeys upon the wall.

The surroundings were disturbingly familiar after the chaos Goriel had seen in other parts of the hulk. He could be on a deck of the strike cruiser a thousand kilometres away, or the battlebarge that had served as his home for much of his time in the 3rd Company. Though ancient and poorly maintained, the ship was proportioned and designed in the Imperial style. As he stood watch, guarding a junction that turned towards the main dorsal corridor, Goriel half expected to see more of his battle-brothers advance around the corner, ghosts of the long-dead crew.

'A few systems are still being powered by the reactor,' announced Lorenzo. 'Most of the primary functions are still working. Life support, power output, engines, all on standby.' There was a pause and then Lorenzo gave a sigh of success. 'This vessel is called the *Wrath of Baal.*'

'*Wrath of Baal*?' echoed Calistarius. 'I know of this ship.'

'We should move to a more defensible position,' said Lorenzo, cutting short any explanation by the Librarian. The squad advanced towards the centre of the ship, Lorenzo guiding them with the aid of the sensorium.

'Find the chapel,' said Calistarius as they descended an open stairwell, the metal of the steps thundering with the crash of their boots. 'The *Wrath of Baal* was lost in the warp thousands of years ago, when the Imperium was born. What few records remain tell of an important cargo, brought from Terra shortly after the traitors' defeat.'

'What cargo?' asked Valencio.

The stairwell brought them onto a wide landing with corridors branching off at right angles in three directions. Calistarius remained quiet while the squad organised themselves. From the contacts on the sensorium data, they were moving closer to another concentration of genestealers.

'The chapel is ahead,' said Lorenzo, indicating the corridor that led towards the bow of the ship. Goriel took up the point position and led the squad forwards. 'Why would we seek cargo in the chapel, and not the hold?'

'The *Wrath of Baal* carries an artefact of great value, although exactly what it is, I do not know,' replied the Librarian. 'That we can feel it, sense its presence, speaks of its importance. Many relics were carried away from the fighting and kept safe in stasis chambers in the reclusiums of the ships: banners borne by our greatest heroes, revered remains, antiquities related to the Angel.'

Genestealers were now closing in from several directions, their forces numerous but divided. Goriel pressed ahead quickly, eager to discover the nature of the artefact that resounded so deeply within his soul.

On Lorenzo's instructions, Zael broke off from the squad and headed to the right, where he would be able to use his flamer to cut off one of the enemy's approaches. The sergeant directed Valencio and Claudio to the left, towards an antechamber on the approach to the main chapel. The others headed towards the reclusium as directly as the network of corridors would allow.

The first of a new wave of genestealers broke from the darkness as Goriel entered a small sanctuary room. The flaking remains of wooden benches lined the walls and scraps of material lay amidst golden rings, the remains of banners that had once been hung with pride upon the walls.

Goriel opened fire, the explosive bolts of his weapon decapitating the first genestealer and ripping apart the chest of the second. A third entered the room and Goriel sidestepped to his right, still firing. Lorenzo came up beside him and the two Terminators cut down several more aliens as they crowded into the narrow doorway ahead.

Beyond the bloodied remains, Goriel could see a large doorway, decorated with a relief design of the Blood Angels' Chapter symbol. Seeing it sent a burst of energy through Goriel and he stormed forwards, crushing the genestealers' bodies underfoot.

'Watch to the left,' ordered Lorenzo. Goriel snapped out of his sudden mania and turned just before the chapel doors as more genestealers came leaping up through an open conveyor shaft. As their claws scraped for purchase, Goriel emptied the remainder of his magazine into the aliens, hurling their bodies back into the dark depths from which they had erupted.

Lorenzo turned to the right and Calistarius moved up between the two Terminators to examine the door.

'It has an intact seal,' the Librarian said.

'Can you open it?' asked Goriel. 'We must get inside.'

'The ciphers of these locks were usually lines from one of the battle litanies,' said Calistarius. He began to punch sequences into a keypad beside the door. The first and second were answered by a flashing red light, and a warning klaxon began to blare through the corridors.

More genestealers charged towards the squad, to be met by a hail of fire from Goriel. This close to the chapel, and the mysterious artefact within, the Space Marine heard every exploding round as a martial drumbeat, crashing in time with the beating of his hearts. The sensation was almost overwhelming. With a clank of hidden bars falling into place, the door to the chapel opened behind him.

'I was right,' said Calistarius. 'It was, "Dedicate your blood to the service of mankind".'

The energy flowing from within the vault hit Goriel like a thunderbolt. Like a river bursting its banks, pent-up hatred and righteous fury filled the Terminator. The urge to slay engulfed him, even as his body and soul were infused with rending pain.

* * *

00.32.88

Valencio poured fire into a stream of genestealers surging through the junction ahead of him. Flashes of lightning exploded around the corner from where, just out of sight, Claudio cut through those aliens that survived Valencio's deadly bursts of fire.

Suddenly a sensation struck Valencio with all the force of a battle cannon shell. For a moment his mind was swamped with a single vision. It was of Sanguinius, Primarch of the Blood Angels. The Angel lay bleeding and broken upon a floor writhing with molten, screaming faces. His wings were tattered and red-stained feathers littered the floor around him. His gold and red armour was gouged and split and his white robes soaked with gore. Great wounds upon his arms and chest seeped crimson and tears of blood streamed down the primarch's beatific face. A shadow loomed over the Angel, amorphous and brooding, utterly black and evil. Pain raged through Valencio. His body felt rent in a dozen places as he shared the agony of his primarch. Countless voices sang out in Valencio's ears, a heavenly requiem both beautiful and chilling.

As forcefully as it had begun, the vision passed and Valencio found himself down on one knee, a genestealer rushing towards him. He pulled up his storm bolter and fired just as the creature tensed to leap, the spray of bolt shells punching the genestealer from its feet. Standing, Valencio pumped two more shots into the writhing alien.

A wordless shout, full of anger and grief, roared over the comm. Valencio turned to see Goriel advancing across a junction, his storm bolter spewing a continuous stream of fire. He passed out of sight, heading towards a large knot of contacts on the sensorium. Lorenzo was shouting also, ordering Goriel to remain in position.

'Recover the artefact, protect the Brother-Librarian,' the sergeant ordered. Valencio saw Lorenzo following Goriel along the corridor and then he too disappeared from view.

'Regroup at the chapel,' Calistarius commanded. Turning to check on Claudio, Valencio saw his fellow Terminator advancing towards him, his armour caked in the drying gore of slain genestealers. Even with the massive enclosing suit of Tactical Dreadnought armour, Claudio looked strangely hunched. He said nothing as he passed, though Valencio could guess his dark thoughts for he shared them.

When Valencio arrived at the chapel doorway Zael, Claudio and Deino had set up a defensive ring, Calistarius between them. The Librarian's sword was sheathed and in his hand he held a large golden goblet. The chalice's cup was moulded in the shape of a skull with the top sliced off. It glowed with a bloody light from within and, as Valencio approached, he could feel the waves of power emanating from the artefact.

'What is it?' Valencio asked.

'A relic of Sanguinius,' Calistarius replied reverentially. 'His blood was once held in this vessel. I can feel it, the provider of our gene-seed indelibly marked the goblet.'

With a closer look, Valencio saw that the chalice was no mere ornament. The silvery metal within its bowl was etched with exquisitely fine lines like a circuit board, each coloured the rusty red of dried blood. There was something disturbing about the patterns cut into the cup and Valencio turned his gaze away.

'We have to find Sergeant Lorenzo,' he said. A cursory examination of the sensorium showed that he was already several dozen metres away, a swarm of genestealers circling his position.

'Negative,' replied the Librarian. 'We must take the chalice to safety and rejoin the main attack.'

'We cannot abandon the brother-sergeant,' said Valencio. 'He needs our assistance. We must protect him!'

'You have served him well, and owe him no further debt,' said Calistarius, not unkindly. 'You best continue to serve his memory by aiding in the destruction of the enemy.'

'What about Threxia?' Valencio demanded. 'Lorenzo did not abandon me then, and I'll not repay the saving of my life with apathy.'

'Enough,' said Calistarius, and his tone invited no further protest. 'Our absence has already jeopardised the safety of our brothers. We will join them as soon as possible.'

Snapped into obedience by centuries of training and the sharp voice of the Librarian, Valencio pushed aside his guilt and focussed upon the task at hand. More genestealers were moving aboard the *Wrath of Baal* and there was nearly half a kilometre separating the squad from the rest of the Blood Angels.

00.32.81

The brood was suffering. The red hunters had turned the air to poison in some of the tunnels and trapped the broodlord's progeny. It felt them die. They choked as their organs burned and their skin blistered. They fought without fear but this new weapon could not be killed. The broodlord knew that the others of its kind were helpless, locked in biological stasis. The brood had to protect the others while they resuscitated. All other matters were secondary to survival. It sent a psychic command, organising the brood to concentrate their numbers on the protection of the dormant thousands. Dozens of its progeny following, the broodlord headed towards the hunters.

* * *

00.33.09

Lorenzo fired as the genestealers broke off their attack and slipped back into the darkness. He fought the urge to pursue them, knowing that he would never catch the fleet aliens. He looked about for Goriel and saw his massive form lying halfway through a doorway. Lorenzo crossed the corridor slowly, his armour battered and scored in many places, leaking lubricant fluids. He shuffled forwards with a slight limp, the actuators in his left knee seized.

'Goriel?'

There was no response from the prone Terminator. When Lorenzo reached him, the sergeant found out the cause. Goriel's helm was missing, as was his head. The ragged stump of his neck protruded from the lip of his armour, his enhanced blood forming a thick scab over the wound even though he was dead.

Lorenzo slumped against the frame of the door, dazed and bewildered. So much had happened so quickly he had been caught in a whirl of events that left him confused. There had been the psychic flash of Sanguinius's death pouring through his mind, and then Goriel had set off on a rampage, possessed by some intractable rage. Lorenzo had followed him through the decks of the *Wrath of Baal* towards the engine room. The genestealers had cornered them there, and Lorenzo had thought for the first time in six hundred and fifty years that his time to die had come. An alien's bite had severed the sensorium relay in his helm and his scanners had fallen dead. He had no map and no warning if they returned.

'Command, this is Lorenzo,' he spoke into the comm. There was no reply and he tried again. He switched the receivers to an all-frequency setting and scatters of comm traffic came to his ears.

'Squad Delphi has been eliminated, Squad Gideon to intercept.'

'Main force casualties at thirty-two per cent. Kill ratio falling.'

'Need reinforcements, Triton sector.'

'Ammunition resupply request, Sergeant Adion.'

There were other noises too: shouts of pain, battle cries and warriors dying. Sometimes static would sweep the net, or an inhuman hiss would sound as a genestealer killed a Space Marine as he was transmitting. Gunfire echoed from the helm's communicator, but all around Lorenzo was deathly silence.

He pushed himself upright and limped forwards, away from the engine room. He could remember the way back from the *Wrath of Baal*. After that, his recollection of the space hulk was vague. He hoped that sight would bring recognition and remembrance.

He had reached the upper deck of the Blood Angels ship when his suit lamps failed. Brother Auletio had patched up the power relays in his backpack, but now the suit was draining rapidly and was shutting down systems to maintain movement and life support. With only his auto-senses to guide him, Lorenzo pressed onwards, exiting the *Wrath of Baal* into the wide chamber outside.

He moved away from the windows, back the way they had come. Passing into the tunnels, the darkness thickened again, devoid of all light. He switched to a thermal image, but there was little enough heat reflected from the walls and floor and he frequently stumbled into the edges of doorways or crashed into corners he could not see.

Despite his superhuman body, Lorenzo had lost a lot of blood and the after-effects of the genestealers' psychic attack combined with the overwhelming surge of energy from the chapel were still affecting his mind. Flashes like retinal after-images plagued him as he tried to press onwards. Inhuman, snarling faces crowded into his vision, to be replaced by the mournful sight of the dying primarch. The visions blurred with memories six centuries old. He saw battle-brothers dead for six hundred years fighting for their last moments once again. Lorenzo heard the vox-chatter of that old battle, mixed with communications from his present comrades. Present and past blurred together.

Brother-Captain Thyrus bellowed orders even as a genestealer tore off his arm. Brother Capulo fired his storm bolter into the gaping maw of an alien while another plunged dagger-like claws into the lenses of his helm.

With a crash Lorenzo walked into a wall and fell to one knee. He shook his head, trying to clear his thoughts, to concentrate on reaching the others.

Lorenzo watched Brother-Sergeant Vienis chop apart a genestealer as he shouted for Lorenzo to retreat. The enemy were everywhere. They leapt from shadowy doorways and dark ventilation ducts. Like a swarm of insects, they congregated on the Blood Angels, pulling them down one-by-one, heedless of their own mounting casualties.

'Squad Eristhenes, secure your flank.'

'This is Captain Raphael, target point for toxin dispersal located.'

'Kill ratio rising, we need more ammunition.'

Trying to wrest reality from memory, Lorenzo took a step forward and found that there was no ground beneath his foot. He tipped forwards, overbalanced, and smashed down a stairwell, chunks of plascrete flying from the walls and steps. He landed with a crash, the floor beneath him cracking with the impact, his left shoulder seizing up.

The Terminators fared no better than the other battle-brothers. Their storm bolters jammed with constant firing. They used their heavy flamers to burn the genestealers from each other's backs, the sacred red livery of their comrades blistering and peeling in the flames. Clawed fiends erupted from loose decking plates and dragged warriors down into the darkness. Assault cannon fire cut down swathes of enemies before the weapons exploded from the strain. More and more genestealers poured on.

'Techmarine support not viable at this time.'

'Use the flamers, use the flamers!'

'Squad Gideon, hold your position at all costs.'

Lorenzo staggered to his feet, an unspoken prayer to the Angel on his lips. He dropped his storm bolter, the mechanical relays of his fingers spasming as power surged intermittently along his arm. He fell to his knees and clawed around in the darkness seeking his weapon. Pulling free his power sword, he activated its blade and by the harsh blue light located his gun.

By the light of the power sword he found himself at the bottom of a stairwell. A web of distorted corridors stretched away in four different directions. Everything was slightly twisted, the vessel's whole structure turned out of alignment by the strange torques and tides of the warp.

'Back to the landing zone, retreat!'

Lorenzo blinked, unsure whether the order had been real or imagined. Had something happened? Was the current action going as badly as the first? He turned awkwardly and sat, resting his back against the foot of the steps.

He could not be scared, he could not grieve, but Lorenzo felt an emptiness growing inside him. Isolation crowded into his senses. He sheathed his sword to conserve its power and allowed the darkness to engulf him once more.

His armour would lose motor functions in two hours at the current rate. He had enough life support power for several more hours. Perhaps the others would find his body when they swept the space hulk after wiping out the genestealers; perhaps he would asphyxiate before the genestealers found him if his brothers did not succeed; perhaps he would be granted an honourable death at the hands of an enemy, one last chance to inflict the Emperor's hate upon his foes; perhaps his body would be atomised as the strike cruisers bombarded the space hulk to ensure the destruction of the genestealers. Whatever happened, his destiny was not in his hands any more.

There was nothing more he could do. He was lost and alone, and he had failed. Just like last time, he had failed. Lorenzo powered down his systems and waited for death.

00.40.96

Lorenzo blinked open his eyes, realising that he had fallen into a catalapsean coma. Part of his brain had rested while the other kept watch. Now he had woken but he could not recall what had stirred him. Boosting power to his auto-senses, he looked up.

Something indistinct but definitely real flitted past the end of a corridor. It was a pale shimmer of heat, barely registering. Then came another, and another. They were unmistakably genestealers, all moving in the same direction. Not one of the creatures spared Lorenzo a glance.

Then something larger stalked into view. It was similar in form but almost twice as tall and broad. It paused for a moment and turned its bulbous head in the sergeant's direction. Eyes flared in the darkness and Lorenzo remembered the alien presence that had knocked him unconscious. In a moment the creature broke its hypnotic gaze and moved on.

Disgust welled up from the pit of Lorenzo's stomach. He remembered his helplessness as the alien had invaded his mind. He could almost taste its presence, tainting his spirit, corrupting his body. The anger mingled with self-loathing as he realised how close he had come to giving up.

He had not failed yet, not while he could still fight.

Lorenzo stood up, the power grid of his suit flaring into life. Checking his weapons, he set off after the genestealers. They might be heading towards his brothers or fleeing them; he did not care. He wanted revenge on the creature that had defiled him, that now embodied Lorenzo's abhorrence for these aliens. He would kill that thing or die in the attempt. Nothing else mattered.

00.42.10

The environment systems chamber was a hive of activity. Monotask servitors of flesh and metal lumbered into position with large canisters of nerve toxins on their backs, while Techmarines fussed over an elaborate and anarchic sprawl of tanks, pipes and valves. The air thrummed with power as extra generators were brought in to boost the life support system's own fluctuating energy supply.

'Squads Gideon and Deino will form the last line of defence,' Captain Raphael instructed over the comm. 'All other squads to form perimeter.'

The Techmarines were filing out of the room followed by their servitors.

'Contamination sequence initiated. Predict completion in eight minutes and thirty-two seconds,' Raphael continued. 'Beholden to our honour, prepare for death.'

Gideon turned to his squad, including Claudio who had requested that he replace Omnio. Deino and his warriors were also close at hand. The marksman was quiet, perhaps unsure of his field promotion to fill Lorenzo's position. As the senior combatant present, Gideon felt it was his duty to lead with precision and determination.

'This is the moment of our victory,' he told the Terminators. 'In eight minutes, enough gas will have been pumped into the system to kill all of the dormant genestealers. After that, it is just a matter of clearing out the few thousand already awake. The toxin must reach the required concentration to be fatal. No enemy is to pass us. There must be no damage to the control station.'

'Just leave it to me,' said Zael. 'I'll burn anything that gets inside the room.'

'Negative,' said Gideon. 'The pumping equipment and air ducts are fragile and we cannot risk collateral damage from heavy weapons fire. That goes for you too, Leon. A catastrophic misfire could do more damage than any gene-stealer's claw. Command says no heavy weapons to fire into or out of the environmental control room. Confirm?'

Leon grumbled something about having nothing to use except harsh language, but nodded in compliance.

'The cleansing fires of absolution will be put to good use elsewhere,' said Zael.

Gideon and Deino dispersed their squads, arranging two layers of a defensive cordon around the control room. Gideon glanced at the chronometer and then the sensorium. The genestealers had been massing for several minutes, attacking in small numbers to keep the Terminators occupied. The swathe of green at the edge of the sensorium, about two hundred metres distant, grew thicker and thicker as more genestealers surrounded the Blood Angels.

'Here they come,' someone announced over the comm. The green smudge of the sensorium contracted rapidly and soon the corridors rang with the din of battle being joined.

Gideon had placed himself not far from the only doorway into the control room, Claudio a few metres away at another junction. Their role was to act as a last line of defence should the genestealers break past the guns of the others.

The seconds seemed to tick past slowly, and Gideon forced himself to ignore the chronometer display. He adjusted the grip on his thunder hammer and listened to the combat reports over the comm. The genestealers were rushing forward in a great mass, overwhelming squads with their numbers, pushing on to the next point of defence without pausing. The fighting had rapidly become splintered through the corridors and rooms surrounding the control chamber as some parts of the line broke and others held. The Terminators' kill rates soared, but the Space Marine casualties also slowly mounted.

From further along the corridor, Leon's assault cannon erupted into life with a distinctive roar. Gideon powered his thunder hammer and its sculpted head glowed into life.

The genestealers were through the outer perimeter.

00.46.03

'Estimate contamination complete in four minutes and forty,' Raphael announced.

Deino paid the comm-link little attention, needing to focus all of his attention on the task at hand. Valencio was protecting the right flank, his storm bolter blaring almost constantly as a stream of genestealers surged from ruptured maintenance ducts beneath the deck above.

Deino found the role of sergeant distracting. He was forced to monitor the wider fight, unable to concentrate wholly on his own performance. He snapped off shots at aliens that had outflanked Valencio through a pitted waste disposal pipe whilst checking the sensorium to ensure that Zael was still holding back the alien tide attacking the forward line. The din of the assault cannon just to the left was equally distracting and Deino began to appreciate just how valuable Lorenzo's experience had been to the squad.

'Pull back to your second position, Zael,' Deino ordered, seeing a cluster of contact blips gathering to circumnavigate the Terminator's location. 'Valencio, cover Zael's withdrawal.'

Valencio moved forward as Deino took up the firing position covering the maintenance vent breach while Zael let loose another burst of flame and then retreated in the vital seconds allowed by the barrier of fire.

'Avenge Lorenzo!' shouted Valencio. 'Anoint his memory with the blood of our enemies!'

'Hold position,' growled Deino, seeing that in his battle fervour, Valencio was taking steps forward, exposing his back to attack.

Three blips appeared behind Valencio and the warning was too late. They converged on his signal and then suddenly it went dead. Two of the contacts turned and headed towards Zael.

'Blood of Baal,' spat Deino, caught between two conflicting courses of action. He could move forward and protect Zael's flank, or continue to guard the access route from the higher deck. What would Lorenzo have done?

Deino held his place, blasting apart the chitinous bodies and swollen heads of the genestealers crawling from the maintenance hatches. The mission – to protect the control room – was the primary concern. Zael would have to be a painful but necessary sacrifice.

'Brother Deino!' Gideon called over the comm.

'What?' demanded Deino, frustrated by yet another interruption to his composure.

'Check your sensorium. Flanking force ten metres to your right,' the sergeant calmly told him.

Deino looked and saw that Gideon was correct.

'My thanks, brother-sergeant,' Deino said, backing along the corridor so that he could cover this fresh attack. 'You guard my shoulder as well as the Angel.'

Gideon's reply began with a short laugh.

'Aye, and I'll–' Suddenly there was a grunt of pain and Gideon's signal went dead.

The genestealers were breaking through in three places now, and the survivors of Squads Gideon and Deino were struggling to contain them. Deino repositioned himself once more, turning to look at Claudio at the far end of the corridor. Now he and Deino were the last defenders between the genestealers and the atmospheric ducts.

Claudio was surrounded by aliens, his lightning claws carving flickering patterns of sparkling blood and electricity in the air. Deino could spare him no further thought as more aliens sped across a T-junction ahead and sprinted towards him. He switched to full auto, eschewing the ideals of the marksman in the desperate circumstances. His bolts ripped through the clutch of genestealers, blasting them apart at close range.

A cry from Claudio caused Deino to turn. The Terminator was engulfed by a biting and clawing mass and he fell to his back under the speed and weight of their assault. Deino fired, explosive ammunition stitching wounds across the genestealers and Claudio's armour. The Assault Terminator pushed himself to his feet. Then something hit Deino in the back and he pitched forward, his shots blowing apart the ceiling and causing a tangle of mesh and cables to fall into the corridor.

Deino forced himself to his knees and ignored the genestealer battering his back and shoulders. Beyond the crackling morass of wires and pipes, he saw Claudio fall down again, genestealers leaping past, headed for the control room.

Failure burned in Deino's heart as a clawed hand punched the side of his helmet.

00.48.66

Through a mist of blood, Deino saw the genestealers dashing down the corridor ahead, nothing between them and the toxin vats.

A moment later, he felt the weight lift off his back and the bloodied remnants of the genestealer splashed onto the decking in front of him. More bolt detonations exploded among the advancing aliens, gouging great holes in their flesh, shattering bones and carapace. A figure limped past, a blazing storm bolter in one hand, a glowing power sword in the other. The Terminator fired off another salvo and then turned to look down at him.

'On your feet, brother, there's more fighting to be done,' Sergeant Lorenzo's voice barked from his helmet speakers.

00.48.73

The combat was a blur of anger and pain for Lorenzo. He stood at the door to the Techmarines' poison tanks and gunned down or chopped apart everything that appeared in front of him. The sergeant overrode his suit's systems to pump power to his arms, sacrificing the life support systems so that he could continue fighting. His limbs felt heavy, his hearts threatened to burst through his fused ribs and his lungs burned with unfiltered air, but Lorenzo kept up his relentless defence. The bodies piled in front of him formed a gory barricade, and he was forced to push them aside to keep his line of fire clear.

'Contamination sequence complete,' Captain Raphael

announced after an eternity had passed. 'Victory is at hand. Redemption. Tomorrow, we take the names of the fallen.'

The genestealer assault quickly lessened, and then the attacks ceased altogether. It took a while for Lorenzo to realise the immediate danger had passed.

'Early analysis indicates ninety-eight per cent enemy fatality quotient,' Captain Raphael announced. 'The vengeance of the Blood Angels is ours. Strike hard and strike swift for our final victory.'

'I need a comms-patch,' Lorenzo announced over his external address system, his comm net still malfunctioning. Deino opened a panel on his left arm and drew out a coiled cable, which he plugged into the side of Lorenzo's helmet.

'Boosting your signal now, brother-sergeant,' Deino's voice crackled in Lorenzo's ear.

'Brothers, I have important news,' said Lorenzo.

'Continue, Sergeant Lorenzo,' Captain Raphael replied over the comm.

'Whilst separated I observed a foe the likes of which we had not seen before,' said Lorenzo. As he spoke, Calistarius emerged around the corner of the corridor. Like the others, his armour was heavily damaged, its paint scratched, the ceramite cracked and split and stained with gore. 'I believe it was the same creature that rendered my squad helpless with its psychic attack. It was larger, faster than the rest. I had the sense that it was some kind of leader, co-ordinating the genestealers.'

'Very good, Lorenzo,' said Raphael. 'It is imperative that we locate and destroy this creature. Life scan reports show no anomalies. The sensorium data offers us no discerning information.'

'Perhaps I can assist,' said Calistarius. 'I felt a presence when I came upon the victims of the psychic attack. At the time

I thought it only a residue of assault, but it may be something else, something I can trace.'

'What do you need?' said Raphael.

'Only a moment with Sergeant Lorenzo,' replied the Librarian.

Calistarius stood in front of Lorenzo and laid a hand upon the top of the sergeant's helm. Lorenzo felt a warmth in his mind as the Librarian extended his soul to join with the sergeant's. Suddenly there was a flash of memory and Lorenzo gasped. He was fixed by two pinpoints of light, staring helplessly at the glowing orbs.

Remember. Calistarius's gentle voice appeared inside Lorenzo's skull.

The sergeant's vision drew back from the lights and he saw the creature's snarling face. The scene replayed in his mind, rewinding through the milliseconds that had led up to the psychic attack. He saw the creature in full. It was massive, taller even than the Terminators, an enormous version of the other aliens. Lorenzo could feel its alien intelligence directed towards him, seeping through him.

Awake.

Lorenzo started from his trance and glanced around. His eyes settled on the Librarian in front of him. Lorenzo took a deep breath, his thoughts still muddled. His traumatic episode in the depths of the space hulk resurfaced briefly, a torrent of battle-brothers slain and vicious aliens. Lorenzo fought to control the clashing images and thoughts crowding into his mind.

'I can lay those memories to rest, if you wish,' said Calistarius, sensing the sergeant's unease.

'No,' Lorenzo replied after a moment's thought. 'We must remember the fallen so that we might avenge them. I grow stronger through the adversity of battle.'

'Very well,' said the Librarian. 'When we return to the

Chapter, you and I shall spend some time with the Chaplains. You have carried your grief and fears for six centuries, and the time comes soon when you can let them go. It is not good that you burden yourself with this anguish for so long.'

'Can you locate the aberration?' Raphael interrupted.

Calistarius released his grip on Lorenzo and stepped back. The Librarian held his hand to his helmet and bowed his head. His psychic hood, a tracery of wires and cables framing his helm, burned with power for a moment and motes of energy danced around the Librarian's head. His hand fell to his side and the lights faded. Calistarius seemed to slump in his armour.

'I can,' he said, his voice laboured. 'There is a psychic bond between the genestealers and their leader. Almost familial, patriarchal. There are two more of them close to where Lorenzo made contact. I can feel them now, like a pulsing in the stream of the aliens' mind-web. They are dormant but wakening.'

'We have little force to spare for the hunt,' said Raphael. 'Sergeant Lorenzo, assemble a squad from your brothers at hand and assist Brother Calistarius. We need to contain these unknown life forms, take tissue and destroy them. I will despatch Techmarine assistance to your position.'

'Affirmative,' said Lorenzo, pleased that there was a definite course of action for him to follow after the strangeness of the last minutes. 'Squads Gideon and Lorenzo, assemble at my position.'

As the Terminators gathered, Lorenzo saw that they were in bad shape. The desperate defence of the toxin vats had taken its toll. Deino was clearly suffering, his helmet punctured, blinded in one eye. Valencio was missing the lower part of his right arm, his Tactical Dreadnought armour boosting his superhuman system to seal the wound. Noctis and Scipio were both currently weaponless and the stiffness with which they moved indicated severe damage to the internal systems of their suits. Gideon had lost his storm shield and the field around his thunder hammer glowed dimly from power shortage. Others had comparable states of armour damage and physical injury.

'We need maximum firepower and close assault punch with as few warriors as possible,' Lorenzo told them. 'Brother-Librarian Calistarius will guide us and I will lead the squad. Zael and Leon, your heavy weapons are coming with me. The main force will suffice with storm bolters. Gideon, Noctis, Deino, Valencio and Scipio, return to the staging area for repair and rearmament. Gideon, form an execution squad and report to the captain for the sweep pattern. Claudio, I need you to come with me.'

None questioned the veteran sergeant's judgement. As those who were not coming on the hunt turned to leave, Gideon stopped next to Lorenzo. The others paused and gave such salutes as their damaged armour and grievous wounds allowed.

'You make us all proud to be Blood Angels, brother,' Gideon said with a nod.

'I am proud to serve the Chapter,' said Lorenzo. 'It is an honour to fight alongside such courageous and unflinching brothers. This day you have healed a wound left too long. Whatever happens, fight no more with shame, but with hearts dedicated anew to the glory of the Angel.'

'You also, Lorenzo,' said Gideon. The sergeant looked at the rest of his ad hoc squad. 'What is your duty?'

'To serve the Emperor's Will!' they chorused in reply.

'What is the Emperor's Will?'

'That we fight and die!'

'What is death?'

'It is our duty!'

Still chanting, they marched away.

* * *

00.50.80

'Comms check complete, sensorium check complete,' Lorenzo announced. The signal bar in his helm display was weak but constant, and the steady pulsing of the scanner was clear in his helm display, showing the positions of the other Terminators. He turned towards the Techmarine who had fixed his helm. 'Thank you, brother.'

'You can repay me with a simple service,' said the Techmarine. He held up a strange claw-like device, much like the reductor Apothecaries used to extract the progenium glands from fallen Space Marines. It was connected to a vial coiled with thin piping. 'Before you destroy these unidentified life forms, we want you to take a tissue sample for analysis. We need to determine their origins and vulnerability to the toxins unleashed. It is self-working. Simply activate the rune whilst holding the claw against the creature's flesh.'

Lorenzo took the device and placed it in one of the containers on his armour's belt.

'And those?' the sergeant asked, pointing towards five cuboid machines servitors had placed along the wall of the corridor. The top side of each cube had a dish-shaped hollow punctured by a lens at its centre.

'Portable power field generators,' the Techmarine explained. 'One for each of you. They will bar all movement, should you need to contain the target before tissue extraction. Each has enough charge to last several minutes but they are not impregnable. A determined foe will break through the field in less than a minute.'

'I understand,' said Lorenzo.

'They will also block your own movement and lines of fire, so position them wisely,' the Techmarine warned.

'Affirmative,' said Lorenzo, eager to get moving. 'Anything else?'

'The Angel blesses your endeavour,' said the Techmarine. He gave a thumb up signal and stepped away.

Lorenzo turned to Calistarius and waved a hand towards the Librarian.

'Lead on, brother.'

00.51.23

They had passed the elevator shaft where Lorenzo's squad had first been subjected to the psychic attack and the sensorium was strangely clear. Worryingly clear, Lorenzo admitted to himself. Since the gas attack, the genestealers had dispersed across the inhabitable parts of the space hulk and squads were erecting power field barriers and hunting down the scattered survivors. The only thing that showed on the scanners was an indistinct blob, registering the dormant life signs of the creatures Calistarius had detected. It seemed inconceivable that more of the aliens had not found their way to this area.

'We must hurry, brothers,' said the Librarian. 'I feel the consciousness of these beasts rising to wakefulness.'

The squad pressed on as quickly as their damaged systems would allow, passing across the ruptured hold of a large cargo ship. Claudio was in the lead, Calistarius directly behind him. As soon as the pair stepped through the huge double doors of the storage bay, the sensorium gave a warning tone. There was movement on the periphery of the scanner.

'I hear their call,' said Calistarius. 'Though they are not yet awake, the creatures beckon to their offspring. It is a beacon, and a warning. They know we are here.'

The unidentified life signals were barely two hundred metres away, but there was no straight route to them. The layout of the ship ahead was a confusing mess of overlapping corridors and gantries, pocked with void spaces and inter-laced with narrow crawlspaces and ventilation pipes. Lines of fire would be short and there were numerous entry points for the genestealers to attack. The aliens' numbers were gathering again, converging from other parts of the space hulk.

'Clear fire lanes,' ordered Lorenzo.

Leon took the lead. As he advanced, he opened fire on a sealed door ahead, blowing it from its rusted hinges. He unleashed another burst of assault cannon shells at the next door as he stepped through the wreckage of the first. Something moved in the darkness and he gunned it down without hesitation.

'Zael, secure the left. Brother-Librarian, stay close to Clau-dio,' the sergeant commanded, assimilating the data from the sensorium. The genestealers had learnt well and no longer rushed headlong into the guns of the Terminators. They waited around the corners of junctions and behind the closed doors of rooms sprouting from the network of passages.

'Sealing left flank,' announced Zael. A blue glow lit the corridor as he placed his power field generator on the floor and activated it with his comm-link. 'Power field in place.'

'Push on, clear a path,' said Lorenzo, following closely behind Claudio and Calistarius.

At once, four groups of genestealers rushed forward, closing on the Terminators from every direction. One group was halted on the sensorium and the corridors echoed with the crackle of the power field as the aliens hurled themselves at the barrier placed by Zael. Chain lightning erupted from Calistarius's sword as more genestealers hurtled through a doorway ahead, disintegrating their alien bodies.

As a group, the genestealers fought their way forward. Halfway to the alien life signals, they broke through Zael's power field and a swarm of them surged through the corridors behind the squad. Zael turned and took up a rearguard position, using his heavy flamer to beat back the onrushing tide of aliens.

'I think I see them,' Calistarius announced. 'Yes, there they are, just ahead.'

Lorenzo could spare no time to look for the moment. He let loose bursts of fire at the genestealers coming at the squad from the right, while Leon's assault cannon reaped a harvest of aliens attacking from the opposite direction.

'Swap position, Claudio,' Lorenzo said. A few seconds later, Claudio was by his side. Lorenzo threw down his power field device and activated it, a shimmering wall of blue energy springing up in front of the other Terminator. Content that the rear was protected, the sergeant turned and followed Calistarius.

The Librarian led Lorenzo into a dark room, little more than a storage space between thick pipes that glowed with heat. They were plasma relays for the reactor somewhere below, their warmth sustaining the aliens huddled next to them. The creatures were just like the one that had attacked Lorenzo, giant and obscene. Their limbs were folded against their chests, their ridged heads bowed between the bony plates of their shoulders.

While Calistarius covered the door, alternating between fire from his storm bolter and bursts of psychic lightning, Lorenzo stooped to retrieve the tissue sample needed by the Techmarines. He placed the extractor against a fleshy hump at the base of the nearest creature's neck and activated the device. Its claw flickered out, tearing free a piece of tissue before disappearing into the cooled vial.

At the same moment, one of the creature's clawed hands snapped out and grabbed Lorenzo's arm. It slowly turned its head towards him, its eyes glowing with psychic power.

* * *

00.52.62

Claudio flexed his arms, loosening the fibre bundles in his armour as if they were muscles. A cluster of genestealers clawed and bit at the power field just in front of the Terminator, separated from his wrath by less than a metre's thickness of energy wall. The genestealers were possessed of a manic vigour, throwing themselves at the barrier to get at Claudio.

'Don't be so eager to die,' Claudio growled at the aliens. 'I'm ready and waiting.'

With an explosion of light, the genestealers burst through. In a wave of blue and purple flesh they fell upon Claudio. His lightning claws sent arcs of energy tearing through them even as their blades sliced through flesh and chitin.

00.52.70

Zael checked the load readout on his heavy flamer and saw that he had enough promethium left for two more full bursts. He backed along the narrow corridor as more genestealers clawed their way up through a grille in the floor about twenty metres ahead.

'Not yet,' he muttered to himself.

More genestealers were bursting up through the grating, rushing towards the Terminator.

'Not yet,' he repeated. The first genestealer was barely three metres away when Zael pulled the trigger. White-hot fire filled the corridor, the backblast scorching Zael's armour, his helm display alight with red icons as the armour's cooling systems attempted to compensate. Even so, he felt a sweat break out on his brow.

As the flames licked along the walls and ceiling, and the

bodies of the genestealers popped and cracked, Zael considered his deadly handiwork and smiled.

'One more shot,' he told himself.

00.52.76

Lorenzo's sword was in its sheath at his waist so he fired his storm bolter point blank, the detonations in the creature's body spattering him with chunks of steaming flesh, his auto-senses almost blinded by the proximity of the muzzle flash. The creature's grip remained tight as he tried to pull his arm away and he fired again, blasting apart its skull. Tearing free from its dead grip, Lorenzo turned back towards the doorway.

One moment he was looking at the back of Calistarius's armour as he stood watch, the next moment the Librarian was hauled through the air, crashing against the wall. Something ancient and monstrous unfolded itself in his place, a glimmer of recognition in its alien eyes.

Lorenzo's bolter jammed as he tried to fire, its mechanisms stuck with gory residue from his close-range shot into the bowels of the dormant genestealer. The sergeant raised his sword protectively.

The creature bent down through the doorway, its gaze moving to look at the bloodied remains of the creature Lorenzo had killed. Lips curled back to expose fangs as long as combat knives. The creature hunched, its muscles bunching and cording like thick rope under its dark skin.

Lorenzo braced himself for the creature's attack, even as he sensed movement from the other beast behind him.

A jet of fire engulfed the alien in the doorway, a purifying blast from Zael. The creature shrieked, lunging against the doorframe, buckling the metal with its weight. Promethium was stuck to its body and head, eating away at the flesh. With another scream, it turned and bounded out of sight. A second later Lorenzo heard noises that set his teeth on edge: shattering ceramite, tortured metal, Zael's agonised bawl. Lorenzo had never heard a Space Marine cry out in such a way and he raced to the door.

Zael's remains were scattered across the decking, his blood dripping down through the grillwork. The alien leader was still on fire, lurching from side to side, crashing against the walls of the corridor, leaving dents in the metal bulkheads.

Lorenzo followed it, trying to clear his jammed storm bolter. Ejecting several unfired rounds, he managed to get it working again and raised the weapon to finish off the alien. Some of the promethium had burnt itself out and much of the creature's back and face was a charred mess. Bone and pulsing flesh could be seen through rents in its skin and carapace.

It reached the stop of a stairwell, hunched and limping. Lorenzo fired, the bolt exploding in the creature's lower back. It fell forwards, the metal guard rail of the stairway twisting under its weight.

The creature tipped out of sight, trailing flames, and Lorenzo followed it to the lip of the stairway. The steps descended into darkness for several hundred metres, the creature's body a dimly flickering fire far below.

Reloading his storm bolter, Lorenzo turned around and strode back towards the plasma exchange pipes. There was one more of the beasts to destroy.

00.53.58

'Command, this is Lorenzo. Request plotting of an exit route.'

Lorenzo, Calistarius, Leon and Claudio were advancing

along a narrow walkway that ran around the perimeter of a deep well-like drop. In a haze of red light below the sergeant could see the bulky shapes of plasma reactors. Electricity occasionally arced between damaged generators and leaking gas spumed spasmodically from ruptured conduits.

The sensorium was full of signals, on levels above and below. The genestealers that had been gathering to protect their leaders had now formed into a solid mass, cutting off the squad from the route back to the rest of the Terminators. Now the Blood Angels had to find a way to escape the aliens hunting them through the winding corridors.

'Sergeant Lorenzo,' Captain Raphael's voice cut through Lorenzo's musing. 'Exit point located. External egress, through a venting shaft two hundred metres from your position.'

'External egress, brother-captain?' asked Lorenzo.

'The duct will bring you out onto the surface of the vessel,' Raphael explained. 'Despatching Thunderhawk to your exit location for retrieval. Primary objective is to ensure delivery of the alien tissue sample.'

'Understood, brother-captain,' said Lorenzo. He looked at his sensorium and saw route marker icons flash into view. 'Exit point located.'

'The Angel shall guide your steps, brothers,' Raphael said before cutting the link.

The route took them down two levels and through a network of criss-crossing passageways surrounding the reactor chamber. The genestealers were closing fast on the Terminators' position and Lorenzo calculated that the squad would not reach the venting shaft without contact.

'Leon, rear guard,' he ordered. The taciturn Space Marine responded by lifting his assault cannon in acknowledgement and fell back to the rear of the squad.

They picked their way over a snarled mass of collapsed gantries and ladders and found themselves overlooking another artificial abyss. The venting tunnel was only fifty metres away, down one further level. Escape was close, but Lorenzo allowed himself no thoughts of victory just yet.

00.54.24

Pain. Pain encompassed all of the broodlord's being, body and mind. Physical agony from the burning. Mental torment from the death of its brood. So many killed, the broodmind was but a shadow of its former power. It was spent, a dying force. The broodlord considered hiding, the instinct to survive strong. Reason overruled instinct. The hunters would seek out and slay all of the brood. Survival was not an option.

Blackened skin flaking and cracking, burnt flesh falling in lumps from its bones as it lifted itself to its feet, the broodlord turned its face upward. Its progeny still stalked the hunters. It knew where they could be found. Created as a passionless biomachine, it felt something for the first time since its strange birth. It was a corrupting thought, an emotion that had lurked inside ever since it had contacted the minds of the hunters.

Now it came to the surface, boiling up through the pain, fresh and strong. It was invigorating and for the first time the broodlord understood why the hunters had fought so fiercely. It shared their thoughts. The broodlord clenched and unclenched its claws as it thought about the destruction of its brood and felt this new emotion: hate.

00.54.61

The Blood Angels fought a coordinated retreat towards the exit point. Calistarius and Claudio in the lead, Lorenzo and Leon following behind. They alternated firing and overwatch, cutting through the genestealers ahead and gunning down those that followed behind. They were less than fifty metres from the shaft and safety. Though tough, even the genestealers could not follow the Terminators into the freezing vacuum of space.

The deck ahead had collapsed and piles of crumbling plascrete littered the floor below. The floor they were on was unstable too, and shook every time Leon opened fire. Two ladders led down onto the rubble-strewn deck. Calistarius was the first to swing his weight out onto the corroded rungs bedded into the wall. One snapped under his tread and fell as a small bar of rust into the rubble below. The Librarian lowered himself down while Lorenzo provided covering fire from above. Genestealers were swarming in from behind the squad, above and below, and Lorenzo kept up a steady stream of fire into the exposed corridors beneath him until the Librarian was safely on the ground again.

Calistarius then took up the fight, blasting with his storm bolter, cutting down with his force sword those genestealers that came close enough. Weapons deactivated, Claudio lowered himself clumsily after the Librarian while bolt shells screamed past, picking off aliens waiting below. Once he had a sure footing again, his claws blazed into life and he joined Calistarius to protect the base of the ladders so that the others could descend.

'You first, brother,' said Leon. 'Only one hundred and fifty rounds remaining.'

Lorenzo did not argue and instead sheathed his power sword and hung his storm bolter from his belt. The ladder creaked under the weight of his armour but held strong until he had reached the lower level. The sergeant backed up until he had a view of Leon's position on the upper floor.

'Your turn,' Lorenzo said.

'Negative,' replied Leon. 'Eighty rounds remaining. Insufficient for enemy numbers.'

* * *

00.55.89

Leon turned to face the oncoming genestealers pouring in a swarm from two corridors. He double-checked his ammunition gauge and held his fire. The genestealers circled rapidly, darting in from the left and the right. Leon felt the first leap upon his left shoulder. Another slashed its claws into his back.

'The Angel avenges!' he bellowed, clamping his finger onto the trigger of the assault cannon.

The torrent of shells tore into the ground at Leon's feet, the barrels of the weapon glowing red-hot. The mechanism jammed and the rounds left in the weapon exploded, shearing off Leon's right arm. The resulting detonation engulfed dozens of genestealers and the plascrete beneath them cracked and crumbled. In a huge explosion of dust and rocky shards, the deck collapsed, plunging Leon and the genestealers to a bone-breaking death many metres below.

00.55.98

Calistarius had no time to spare a thought for Leon's sacrifice. Lorenzo approached the Librarian and took the tissue sample from his belt.

'Protect this,' said the sergeant, holding out the device. Calistarius took the sample without comment and turned towards the evacuation point.

'Go with him,' he heard Lorenzo say and Claudio appeared by his side.

The two of them picked their way through the rubble-choked passage, Lorenzo close on their heels. Occasionally they turned to fire at the pursuing genestealers, cutting down any that came within sight.

They were barely ten metres from the venting shaft.

Calistarius could see the maintenance access hatch they needed to break through to get inside.

'I'll watch your back,' volunteered Claudio, indicating to Calistarius that he should cut through the hatchway.

The Librarian turned towards the square door and plunged his force sword into the locking mechanism. He trembled as he allowed his psychic power to surge along the blade, melting the bolts of the lock. With a clang, the hatch fell free, revealing the dark shaft beyond.

Calistarius felt the broodlord before he heard or saw it. Its presence was suddenly there, just behind the Terminators. The Librarian turned in time to see Lorenzo flung out of the alien's path, still firing his storm bolter. The veteran crashed through a half-ruined wall and fell out of sight.

Claudio launched himself at the monstrous creature like a wild cat, his claws severing an upraised limb. The broodlord brought its other three clawed hands together, grabbing hold of Claudio's arms. With sickening twists and wrenches, the genestealer ripped the Terminator's left arm out of its socket. Claudio's right arm snapped in several places despite the protection of his armour.

Not content, the broodlord closed its massive jaws on Claudio's head. A few of its fangs snapped, but some managed to punch through Claudio's armoured helm. Arching its neck and back, the broodlord pulled off the Space Marine's head with its jaws, splinters of eye lenses and ceramite showering to the ground amidst the arterial fountain from Claudio's ravaged body.

Calistarius knew that he should escape. The tissue sample in his belt was more important than the death of a single creature. He was about to turn when the broodlord focussed its alien gaze upon him.

With a shock that stunned his system, the Librarian found his psyche swamped by the malignant power of the brood mind. As it penetrated the psyker's brain, Calistarius felt a jolt of connection with the amorphous thoughts of the genestealers.

Space and time took on a new perspective, all emotion drained from his soul. He was timeless, endless, immortal. One of countless billions, a mote in a hurricane of minds. Fleeting yet eternally reborn. The broodmind linked him to the other things, sharing his thoughts, his hunger, his instinct to reproduce and grow.

But they were not his thoughts. They were alien. Calistarius could not sense where he ended and the broodmind began. He struggled to resist. He felt a tugging on the edge of his personality, a great psychic beacon that flared in every direction. It was like the Astronomican he used to guide ships through the warp, yet far weaker and far fouler. It was a cancer, now small, much reduced by the deaths the brood had suffered.

He realised that far out in the depths of space there were other dark beacons, other broodminds. And something larger. Something that swallowed everything in its path. Something mankind had never seen before. Impossibly distant and impossibly ancient. A shadow in the warp.

The connection broke and Calistarius found himself looking at the broodlord's face, barely half a metre from him. It was transfixed on a glowing blue blade and Calistarius realised the light in the creature's eyes were not of life, but simply reflections from the humming power sword.

Lorenzo pulled his sword free from the creature and it slumped to the ground. The sergeant then proceeded to calmly and methodically chop off its remaining three arms, both its legs and, finally, its head.

'Just to be sure,' Lorenzo explained. His left arm hung

uselessly by his side and he stood with a strange stoop. A warning tone sounded from the sensorium. Another wave of genestealers had been following the broodlord and was now barely twenty metres away.

Lorenzo turned towards them and awkwardly raised his sword. The Librarian sheathed his own weapon and turned to face the sergeant.

'This is victory,' Calistarius said, holding up the tissue sample.

'After you,' said Lorenzo, pointing his sword towards the open exhaust shaft.

The Librarian clambered through the hatchway while Lorenzo opened fire at the approaching aliens.

'Time to leave, sergeant,' said Calistarius.

Lorenzo hesitated, gunning down another genestealer. He wanted to stay and fight. He wanted to kill more of the foe. His every instinct told him not to turn away and leave. It felt too much like a retreat. The Angel had given his life for the Blood Angels and Lorenzo could do no less.

With a parting shot, Lorenzo pushed himself into the exhaust duct.

To live and fight again, to remember the sacrifice made this day and six hundred years ago, that was true victory. To survive and allow the memories to live on when so many had not, that was the ultimate triumph.

There was no failure in that.

00.57.17

SANGUIS IRAE

Peace.

An almost impossible moment for one who had been raised in the hell of Baal's radioactive deserts and who had spent a lifetime waging war against the foes of the Emperor, cursed by psychic powers so that even outside battle there was ever a contest to keep out the clamour of the warp and the minds of his fellow Space Marines.

Here there was nothing. Alone on the boarding torpedo, there was not even a pilot to disturb Calistarius's contemplation. All was still. The torpedo's launch provided enough silent momentum to carry the one-way transport across the few hundred kilometres of void to the Blood Angels Librarian's destination.

No thoughts, no noise, just the barest murmur of background hum from the resonance of the warp itself.

The peace brought clarity.

Calistarius knew better than to fill this moment with distracting thoughts – concerns over the mission he was about to embark upon, ideas of higher philosophies or idle con-templation of the latest Chapter rumours and news.

He focused on himself and nothing else. A mote of life encased in a ferrolene and ceramite cylinder drifting across the vacuum of space, infinitesimally insignificant to the uni-verse. He enjoyed the feeling of pointlessness. For just a few minutes Calistarius was totally freed from care. His righteous burden awaited him, but until the boarding torpedo plunged through the metal skin of the space hulk marked SA-BA-325 he was free from all responsibility and expectation.

His breaths came slowly, inhaling and exhaling in slow rhythm with the beating of his twin hearts, a soft after-shudder in his chest as his third lung inflated with a slight delay. His cardio-pulmonary system was a simple but enchanting quin-tet piece, occasionally accompanied by a solo percussion creak or ping from the hull of the boarding torpedo.

Calistarius had not known music as a child. The closest that the tribes of Baal Secundus came to orchestration was war drums and pyre dirges. It was only when he had passed the trials of the Blood Angels and become a son of Sanguin-ius that young Calistarius had learnt of instruments – of flute and riola, violin and helleschord, pantache and cymbal.

Before that discovery he had never heard the music inher-ent in the universe, not until he had been played symphonies composed to emulate the vast array of nature's moods. He had listened with delight, his mind's ear turning screeching chords to the howl of the Baal winds, the petulant percus-sion of tom-toms converted to the drumming foot beats of a carrion-reaper charging over the dunes.

A gift from the Blood Angels – civilisation. Art in all its forms: poetic, literary, visual and military. The legacy of mighty Sanguinius, that the deformed, radiation-scarred vagrants of the deserts could be lifted above their station and turned into demigods. Not just a physical transformation, but a mental, cultural uplifting as well. To be defenders of humanity one needed not only bolters and power armour, but a sense of what was so important that it required the keenest sacrifice. The boons of giant physique and razor-sharp mind were simply part of the exchange. In return, every Blood Angel would give his life and death in service to the Emperor and the Imperium of Mankind he had created.

A new, harsh sound ripped into Calistarius's thoughts, dragging him out of his reverie. Arrestor engines screamed into life, jolting the torpedo with fierce deceleration for a few seconds before the melta-charges in the tip exploded into life, tearing the hull of the space hulk to allow the energy-shielded prow to punch through.

More detonations followed as the front of the torpedo petalled outwards, forming an air seal and disembarkation ramp. Calistarius was free of his harness and on his feet even before the torpedo had finished moving. The moment the splay of the torpedo's tip was wide enough, he ducked through the opening portal and leapt down to the deck two metres below.

He checked his bearings and located the initial exploratory squad's position on a wrist-mounted auspex. They were about three hundred metres away, deeper within the structure of the hulk where teleportation was far riskier. Calistarius already had his bolt pistol in his left hand. He pulled free a power sword with the right and set off, all senses alert to possible attack.

The clank of his boots echoed harshly from metal bulkheads, ringing strangely from the buckled material of the outer hull. A broken ventilator fan whickered close at hand, letting forth a scraping snarl every few seconds. Something clattered above the ceiling like a spoon rattling against the bottom of a ration tin: an old pump, perhaps.

The thrum of the power blade springing into life added another noise to the mix.

There was no symphony here. No peace.

War had returned.

Calistarius encountered the first of the initial landing squad guarding a cross-junction two hundred metres from where the Librarian's boarding torpedo had breached. Brother Santiago's Terminator armour almost filled the corridor as he turned one way and then the other, his storm bolter held at the ready. Santiago acknowledged his battle-brother's approach with a lifted power fist.

'Nice of you to join us.' Santiago's attempt at humour masked an unease that Calistarius had sensed the moment he had laid eyes on the other Blood Angel. He did not have to be psychic to detect his battle-brother's restlessness.

'The… other warrior, he is still alive?'

'Yes, brother. The strength of Sanguinius must truly flow in his veins, because very little blood does.'

'Then I will not delay here any longer.' Calistarius gave his companion a nod of respect as Santiago stepped aside to allow him to proceed down the corridor.

Closing in on the rest of the squad, the Librarian saw that they had dispersed – two of the Terminators were at the target location beacon on the auspex, while the other two held strategic bottle-necks further along the deck. Calistarius headed straight for the objective location, noting the sensorium transponder signal of Sergeant Dioneas in the same chamber.

There was only one way into and out of the room, until recently sealed tight. The scorched, buckled marks of claws

and lasers marred the door and the wall around the locking mechanism, but override codes had pried open what the
brute strength of the unknown assailants had not.

The inside of the chamber was lit only by the suit lights
of Dioneas and Brother Marciano; the latter stepped away
from the door as he saw Calistarius approaching, allowing
the Librarian to see inside.

The sergeant stood over another figure in bulky Terminator
armour, slumped against the far bulkhead. Calistarius knew
what to expect but still experienced a moment of pause when
he saw the Blood Angels livery painted on the ancient suit of
armour. Worse still were the many gashes in the heavy war-plate.
Much of the suit had been ripped away, the endo-skeletal struts
and fibre bundles twisted and tattered by immense tears.

Dioneas shifted as the Librarian entered and for a moment his
suit light played across the face of the injured Blood Angel. His
mouth was locked in a bestial snarl, lips drawn back to expose
dark gums, eyes glaring, glinting fiercely in the passing light.

In the moment of contact Calistarius felt madness. Deep,
utter hatred and bloodlust surged into the Librarian's
thoughts, pounding upon his mind like hammer blows.

Calistarius closed his mind off in an instant, shielding himself from the sensation as though it were an attack.

'You know what this is?' Dioneas's voice was quiet over
the vox-link.

'Of course,' said Calistarius. 'The signs are obvious. Why
did you request my presence, brother-sergeant?'

'Our initial landing and sweep detected nothing,' the sergeant explained. 'It was only when we were preparing to
expand to a secondary perimeter that we detected the heat
source of his tactical dreadnought suit. This is exactly how
we found him, locked inside this empty armoury magazine.'

'And you wish me to delve into his thoughts?' Calistarius kept his gaze fixed on the sergeant, not willing yet to look at the contorted features of the collapsed Space Marine. 'What do you hope I will find there?'

'Anything,' whispered Dioneas, turning his bulky armour to look at the prone Blood Angel. The suit lights caught the jagged edges of the rips in the adamantium, flared from the shattered plates of ceramite and glistened on exposed flesh and bone. 'Who he is, why he is here, what did this to him.'

'You have no hint of his identity?'

'His suit transponder is dead. No markings, nothing we can use, have been left on his armour.'

'Why have you not transported him back to the battle-barge?'

'Does it look to you that he would survive such a journey?'

'No,' admitted Calistarius. 'What is the current tactical situation? Clearly he was attacked by something.'

'No life signs detected by the primary surveyor sweep and nothing on the sensorium until we found… this.' Dioneas took a step toward the door. 'It will be just the six of us for now. Captain Raphael is not prepared to send in the main wave until we have a better idea of what they might run into. As soon as you can confirm whether there is a credible threat aboard or not, the sooner our reinforcements will arrive.'

Calistarius nodded. 'I shall endeavour to conclude this swiftly.'

The other two Blood Angels left the room. Dioneas stood guard at the door while Marciano moved out further to reinforce the perimeter defence. Calistarius looked at the broad back of the sergeant standing outside for a while, wondering if he should ask him to return. The Blood Angel they had found was in some kind of catatonic coma, but there was no way to predict what would happen when Calistarius began his psychic probing.

'Sergeant,' he said after considering the matter, 'I would prefer it if you kept watch on... on my subject. While I am inside his mind I will be vulnerable if he strikes out.'

'As you wish, brother,' said Dioneas.

When the sergeant stepped back into the chamber the lights of his war-plate glinted from the splintered tines of the fallen Space Marine's lightning claws. There was dried blood – not his own – splashed along their length. Calistarius crouched to examine them more closely.

'I noticed that too,' said Dioneas. 'If his claws had been functioning, the energy sheath would have vaporised any exposed liquid.'

'He carried on fighting even after his claws stopped working,' concluded Calistarius. 'Curious, but not surprising. If he was gripped by... If the gene-curse had possessed him he would have no control over his actions. He would fight until dead.'

'So why is he still alive?'

'Perhaps he killed all his foes?'

'Leaving no evidence of them for us to find?'

'How would he have had the presence of mind to lock himself in here, if the Black Rage had him?'

'You ask the same questions that provoked my call for assistance,' Dioneas said pointedly. He gestured towards the near-dead Blood Angel. '*He* has the answers.'

Reaching out hesitantly, his pistol holstered, Calistarius laid a hand on the mortally wounded Space Marine. He almost flinched at an imagined response, but the dormant Blood Angel did not move, not even a flicker of the eyes. He looked physically dead but there was enough anima left in his Terminator armour to sustain vital functions.

He reached with his mind also, sensing that the soul of

the warrior was still intact. The Librarian had his psychic defences fully prepared. Physical contact was not necessary to dig into the dying warrior's thoughts, but Calistarius hoped the Blood Angel would feel it somehow and gain a sense of comfort before his mind was peeled apart by the Librarian.

Calistarius looked at the mess of armour and torn flesh and pondered Dioneas's analysis. It seemed that the Space Marine was certainly in a state of suspended animation, and the activation of the sus-an membrane could be triggered instinctively at the verge of death. However, the curse, the Black Rage as it was known amongst the Blood Angels, was an all-encompassing bloodthirst. Those who succumbed to the flaw of the Chapter wanted nothing but oblivion, consumed by inner agony and anger. Once the Black Rage took hold of a warrior, death was the only release.

'Who are you?' Calistarius whispered, moving his hand from the broken shoulder plate to the cheek of the fallen warrior. He opened his thoughts and asked the question again, allowing the response to flow back from the inert form of the Blood Angel.

SLAYER!

The raw strength of the Black Rage hit Calistarius and though he had been expecting it, at the moment of contact he shared the deepest loathing and despair that fuelled the warrior beneath his fingers. He wanted to kill until he was killed, uncaring of any other action or fate.

The Librarian wrestled himself free, forming a ball of pure consciousness like ice amidst the flaming maelstrom of anger. The ice was melting slowly as the rage lapped at it, but in turn its presence cooled the surrounding fire, allowing Calistarius to send tendrils of interrogation into the Blood Angel's mind, trickling them in like water.

He encountered memory, and upon examining it relived it as his own.

Aboard the Arch-traitor's battle-barge. The strike force had been scattered and there was no sign of the Emperor or Rogal Dorn. Some of his warriors were with him, nine from his honour guard in scarlet and gilded armour. The communications network was a cacophony of screams and urgent situation reports, overlaid with horrific cackling and demented braying.

A drop of blood fell on his cheek. His eye was drawn up to the ceiling. There was a Space Marine trapped there, inverted, having reconstituted halfway into the material of the ship itself. One leg and arm hung from the metal as his life fluid seeped along lines of rust like artificial veins. He thrashed for a moment and then fell limp.

'My lord!' One of the honour guard was demanding his attention. He dragged his gaze away from the contorted body above. 'What are your orders, Lord Sanguinius?'

It was wrong. These were not real memories. Calistarius pushed through them, ignoring the tide of longing that flooded through him as he touched the soul of Sanguinius and felt emptiness and loss.

The surge of disorientation from teleportation dies away, leaving him in a half-flooded corridor. The rest of the squad are close at hand on the sensorium and the sergeant calls off names to ensure they have all arrived.

'Vespesario?'

'Present, brother-sergeant,' he responds, forging through the thigh-high water towards a broken bulkhead to his right. 'Starting security sweep.'

* * *

'Vespesario,' Calistarius croaked, pulling himself back through the demented ravings that roiled like storm clouds across the other Blood Angel's thoughts. The Librarian looked up at Sergeant Dioneas. 'Brother Vespesario. You should check with the data-cogitators on the battle-barge.'

'No need,' replied the sergeant. He sighed heavily. 'There have been only a few brothers named Vespesario in the history of the First Company. I know which one this is.'

'I also have a recollection of code-name: *Omen of Despair*. A space hulk called *Omen of Despair*.'

'Yes,' said Dioneas. 'It was discovered in the Verium Placus belt near the Ordanio system, two hundred and forty-six years ago. That is nearly seventeen thousand light years away. Two First Company squads went aboard for primary reconnaissance. The wreck unexpectedly dropped back into warp space almost as soon as they boarded. All ten warriors and suits of battleplate were lost, presumed destroyed.'

'But not so,' said Calistarius. 'We must be aboard the *Omen of Despair*.'

'Apparently so.' There was a click as the sergeant changed his vox-channel, presumably to transit this message back to the battle-barge. A few seconds later the click sounded again as he returned to the squad address channel they had been using. 'That answers one question, but it does not tell us what happened, or what we might expect to find. I would prefer not to share their fate.'

Calistarius, armed with this new information as a guideline for his probing, turned his attention back to Vespesario. Everything dropped away as he lowered himself into the turbulence of the Blood Angel's mind. Again the rasping hatred sawed at the Librarian, threatening to cut through his thoughts and infect him with its purity of purpose.

Vespesario.

He fixed on the name like an ancient navigator might choose a star to gain his bearing.

It did not stop the flames lapping again at the Librarian's defences, seeking a way into his inner thoughts, probing his mental strength even as he sought ingress to Vespesario's memories.

As before, there was an outer layer, an ashen, black crust formed from the gene-curse that was bound up in Vespesario's every fibre, now unleashed.

'Send rally signals. All Blood Angels to converge on my position,' he commanded. The order came easily, the need for action sweeping away any vestiges of horror he might have felt. His words, his voice, settled those around him, giving them strength with his presence alone. The honour guard checked their weapons and fell in behind their lord as he surveyed the chamber more closely.

The walls were like nothing he had seen aboard a battle-barge. The power of the warp was in them, creating curves and peculiar organic shapes even as spines of iron jutted with jagged edges and sheaths of plastek slid over light fittings like blinking eyes. The dimensions of the room did not quite fit each other, so that corners seemed higher than the ceiling and walls longer than the floor.

He had not experienced the like on a ship, it was true, but he had encountered the power of the warp many times before, and he was reminded of Signus. Its effect was much reduced. He concentrated, pushing aside the impossibilities. There was a doorway ahead, open to reveal a grandiose hall beyond. He headed for it, calling his sons after him.

There was movement ahead and a moment later the first of the daemons appeared.

* * *

The staging ground is secure, but all contact has been lost with the strike cruiser. The sergeants are holding a brief conversation and soon they announce the outcome of their deliberations.

'We have translated into the warp,' Sergeant Commeos tells them. 'Moments after we teleported aboard.'

'How are we not dead?' asks Geraneos.

'A functioning Geller field,' Vespesario answers, guessing. 'Pure luck.'

'Not so lucky that we are on our own in here,' says Sergeant Adonius. The sensorium lights up with contact warnings. Something is closing on their position. 'Ready your weapons, brothers.'

For a split-second Calistarius was caught between three realities: the *Omen of Despair* in the present; the space hulk more than two centuries earlier; and Vespesario's Black Rage-induced gene-memories of their primarch trapped aboard the Warmaster's starship.

'We have multiple incoming signals.'

It took another three seconds for the Librarian to realise that the words were in his ear, not his mind, spoken by Sergeant Dioneas. He broke away completely from Vespesario, lifting his hand from the near-dead warrior's cheek to check the auspex.

Life signals, fore and aft of their position. They were still half a kilometre distant, approaching slowly but growing in number.

'What are they?' Dioneas demanded. 'What is coming for us?'

Calistarius did not understand why the question had been directed at him. How was he supposed to know what the others did not? Realisation dawned.

Vespesario knew.

He closed his eyes and this time pushed into the flames without wavering.

* * *

At first the daemons were shifting, formless things, drawn to the Space Marines as wisps of bright energy. They circled and danced, never staying still, growing in strength and numbers, flitting past doorways and skimming overhead, not quite coming into the range of power axe or chainsword. A few of the Blood Angels opened fire with bolters and pistols, sparking bursts of detonations against warping bulkheads as they tried to track the flitting apparitions.

'Cease firing, save your ammunition,' he told them.

A constant moaning and screaming accompanied the party as they forged along a corridor of crystal walls, faceted to fragment and disperse the reflections of the legionaries. He glanced at one such image, seeing himself whole for a moment – tall, finely featured, eyes of deep blue, shoulder-length hair. But there was a cruel smile on his lips and wickedness in his gaze as something else looked back at him in mockery. A shift of view, another reflection, of lifeless eyes and half his skull missing, his throat slit. He moved his eyes again and this time saw himself in triumphant ecstasy, eyes filled with crimson, blood dripping from fangs that had split his gums.

He knew nothing of what his companions saw but their disconcerted grunts and whispered curses told him that the visions were not welcome.

The crystal passage brought them to a state room, furnished lavishly with a wood and leather suite of chairs and couches, bookcases on the wall lined with volumes and a table on which sat a decanter filled with a deep purple liquid.

'Touch nothing,' he warned, catching a glimpse of the spines of the books, marked with changing runes in a tongue that was anathema to sanity and reason. 'Read nothing.'

A book fell from a shelf to his right, opening at the image of a screaming child with tentacles erupting from her eyes. One of the Space Marines stooped to look at it and gave a disgusted snarl. As though prompted by this reaction, the image burst into life, tentacles uncoiling out of the pages, whip-fast, around the Space Marine's neck and helm.

Before a shot was fired, the legionary was dragged forward into a gnashing maw where the girl's ruby lips had been, head bitten off by the fanged monstrosity. Tossing aside the decapitated remains, the book-pseudopods grew even longer, seeking a fresh victim.

More books hurled themselves off the shelves, revealing pictures of nightmarish beasts with curling horns, cyclopean figures with ruptured skins and spilling guts, steel-clawed hounds and diamond-eyed succubae. The Blood Angels did their best but could not avoid seeing these demented pictures. Their instinctual fear and revulsion gave life to the magic within, drawing forth the daemons bound within the pages.

In a few seconds the room was full of ghastly foes of mad proportion and terrible purpose. Wailing, screeching and howling, they fell upon the Space Marines with baroque curved blades and dagger-like talons. Battle-cries and shouts of alarm rang out, punctuated by the roar of bolters.

He threw himself into the fray, sword glittering, pulses of plasma from his pistol incinerating the Chaos monsters. As he sliced a red-skinned creature with the head of a goat and the body of a dwarf, his stare fell upon the pages of a book depicting an infinitely deep maw. In a moment the air was being sucked from the room, books whirling, furniture upended by the all-consuming vortex.

With a contemptuous snarl he fired his pistol, turning the book to a blackened mess that bubbled and steamed.

'Press on,' he called to the others, pointing his sword at the vast wooden door at the far end of the room. 'We seek the Traitor.'

Signals were clogging the sensorium data-feed, so that individual life readings were blurring together into a mass of returns a little more than two hundred metres from the perimeter. It was as though the *hulk itself was coming alive, vomiting forth a stream of unidentified foes that were remaining just out of sight and out of reach.*

'What are they?' asks Geraneos. 'Where are they coming from?'

'Secondary ducting,' Sergeant Adonius answers the second question. He offers no opinion on the first. 'Air vents, cable tiers, maintenance access.'

'Fast-moving,' comments Vespesario. 'Biding their time, not simply charging towards us.'

'Perhaps they are afraid of us,' suggests Brother Lucasi. 'That is why they do not attack.'

'What do we do?' Brother Tarantus gives voice to the question that has nagged Vespesario for the last few minutes. 'What is our mission here?'

The silence of the sergeants is disconcerting. The Blood Angels had come to investigate the Omen of Despair *and report back to their captain. Now they were trapped in the warp, most likely to die drifting on the immaterial tides.*

'If there are working Geller fields there could be a operational warp drive,' Sergeant Commeos says eventually. 'We should locate and secure the controls.'

'We stay together,' Adonius adds. His voice gains confidence as he continues to speak. 'We must consider all contacts to be hostile. Emperor alone knows how long this hulk has been drifting, picking up all sorts of infestations and stowaways. Orders are to terminate any life form on sight.'

'My squad will lead,' says Commeos. 'Orthodox sweep pattern alpha. Serrajo takes rearguard.'

The nominated Terminator accepts this duty with a grunt and turns aside as the others continue along the corridor.

They come out in some kind of systems hub: a cavernous vault lined with pipes and cables, a plume of steam gathering around ruptured feedlines. The air is thick with vapour, which catches as droplets on their armour. In the light of the emergency lamps set into the bulkhead, they turn into rubies that slide down the painted ceramite, leaving glittering trails.

The sensorium shifts focus as Serrajo directs his suit's scanners to the rear. The life signs are on the move, gathering behind and to the flanks of the Terminators' line of advance.

'Trying to keep away from us?' says Vespesario, but his question is answered by the readings on the sensorium. The life signs become bright signals of movement as the semi-circle of returns collapses towards the two squads.

'Incoming enemies. Purge them swiftly,' calls Adonius.

The first of the signals reaches the chamber in a shockingly short space of time – scant seconds after the enemy began to close.

'They were here already,' barks Commeos. He lifts his storm bolter and fires up at the ceiling. 'Dormant in the steam cloud!'

A body falls out of the gloom, riddled with bolt wounds, trailing yellow ichor. It has six limbs: two legs, recurved and double-jointed; two upper appendages like tentacles, lined with bony spurs; two other arms each ending in three dagger-like claws. Its head is bulbous and mottled with lumps of moss growth from long hibernation; black, lifeless eyes above a flattened snout and a mouth filled with needle-like fangs. Under dark grey chitin marked with white tiger stripes is purplish flesh tight with muscle and tendons.

Another of the creatures looms out of the darkness towards Vespesario, claws outstretched, mouth opened wide. A tubular tongue glistens with alien fluid.

This one is alive.

'Genestealers!' Calistarius shouted the warning the moment he dragged himself free from Vespesario's memories. 'They are using thermal ducts and power exchanges to mask their hibernation areas. Watch for attacks from sub-ducting beneath the decks.'

'Hold positions, defensive stance,' ordered Dioneas. A click and a buzz heralded his switch to long-range transmission to the strike cruiser.

Calistarius stood up, almost disappointed. Space hulks were known to carry all manner of potential threats, including orks and other aliens, adepts and devotees of the Dark Powers and even Traitor Space Marines. In the last few decades genestealers had become an increasingly prevalent peril, and the Blood Angels had encountered their fair share of the hideous xenos. Only a few years earlier Calistarius had been part of the boarding teams that had cleansed the *Sin of Damnation* of another swarm.

'Standard infestation protocols,' Dioneas continued, having received orders from Captain Raphael. 'We will fall back to the insertion point and establish a breach-head for the incoming second wave. Estimated time to reinforcement is seventeen minutes.'

'What about Vespesario?' asked Calistarius. 'We cannot leave him here.'

'This area is too tight for a solid defensive cordon against a superior close assault foe,' replied the sergeant. 'We need to withdraw to the outer galleries where we have better lines of fire.'

'And abandon one of our own?'

'That is not a Blood Angel.' Dioneas's voice was harsh over the vox as he turned away. 'It is a hunk of meat kept alive by a combination of sus-an membrane and barely functioning armour life support systems.'

Calistarius was about to argue further but the sergeant cut him off, his tone more conciliatory.

'When the secondary wave arrives we shall make this chamber a primary objective. We can secure the area with more warriors and allow the Apothecaries to do their work.'

It was hard for Calistarius to step away. He had shared Vespesario's thoughts and knew that there was something of the Space Marine still inside the broken body and shattered armour. He had made a connection with his battle-brother, though separated by centuries, and owed it to a fellow Blood Angel to ensure the best chance for survival. Vespesario had done all that he could, sealing himself inside this room, and somehow he had endured. Now that the Blood Angels had breached the door there was nothing to stop the genestealers finishing what they had begun so long ago.

Calistarius was also prepared to admit to himself that he was intrigued by the potential of examining the mind of a Black Rage victim in more detail. Normally delving into the thoughts of one of his brothers so deeply would be taboo, especially those beset by the blood curse. It was a unique opportunity to gain an insight into what the victims of the Black Rage experienced and, perhaps, a chance to ease the suffering of others or maybe even take a step closer to a cure.

'Wait, brother-sergeant,' said the Librarian as he was about to step across the threshold. Dioneas was heading away down the corridor and did not stop. 'Why did he lock himself away like this? We have to find out.'

'An easily defensible position to make a last stand against the genestealers,' replied Dioneas, still advancing along the passage. 'Little mystery to be explained, I think.'

'A remarkably rational decision for one gripped by the madness of the Black Rage.'

Dioneas stopped at a junction a few dozen metres ahead and turned back to face the Librarian. 'Your meaning?'

'No plainer than what I have said,' continued Calistarius. 'I do not have an answer to that, but from everything we know he would not retreat and he certainly would not have had the presence of mind to close and seal the bulkhead. Something strange happened here two centuries ago.'

'I agree, and we shall uncover the truth of such events once we have properly secured a breach-head and expanded our cordon.' Dioneas turned away. 'We must withdraw, Brother-Lexicanium.'

Captain Raphael had made it clear before Calistarius had departed that battlefield command fell to Sergeant Dioneas, a veteran of several centuries more than the Librarian. Chapter law demanded that Calistarius obeyed the direct command of his superior, but his every instinct was warning him otherwise. As a psyker, he knew instinct was often an indication of some deeper sense.

When Dioneas realised that the Librarian was not following, he stepped back into view.

'Your orders are clear, brother. The warriors of the Librarium at not immune to censure and punishment. Follow me.'

Calistarius used a sub-vocal command to switch to the command hail channel.

'Captain Raphael? This is Lexicanium Calistarius. I must speak with you urgently.'

'Calistarius?' Raphael's voice was deep and rich, and he spoke calmly despite the unorthodox nature of Calistarius's communication. 'This is the command channel. What has happened to Sergeant Dioneas? His transponder reports normal vital signs.'

'The sergeant is unharmed, captain. We cannot withdraw. Not yet. I must continue my psychic scan of Brother Vespesario. Abort the reinforcement wave until I have completed my probe.'

There was a long pause before Raphael replied.

'Second wave is being despatch in forty seconds. You have thirty to convince me.'

Calistarius quickly told the captain of his suspicions concerning Vespesario's behaviour. Raphael listened without interruption and when the Librarian finished asked a simple question.

'Are you willing to stake your honour and good name on this... instinct?'

There was no doubt in the Librarian's mind. It was some unfocused warning from his psychic sense, a warp-powered intuition that made it more than a simple hunch. 'Absolutely, brother-captain. Delay the reinforcement wave for five minutes, that is all I ask.'

'Very well, you have five more minutes.'

The vox-link broke into static for a couple of seconds and then went quiet. Another few seconds passed before Dioneas spoke up, during which the sergeant received fresh orders from the captain.

'You circumnavigated the chain of command, brother,' the sergeant growled, advancing back along the corridor towards Calistarius. 'You are placing yourself and our battle-brothers in great danger. We cannot hold this position for five minutes if the genestealers attack. I urge you to reconsider.'

'I will not, brother-sergeant,' said Calistarius. 'I cannot. I am prepared to wager our six lives against the ninety more that will be risked should the second wave be launched.'

'Your five minutes have already begun,' the sergeant said, pointing at Vespesario with his power sword. 'Use the time wisely.'

The Librarian said nothing as he returned to Vespesario's inert form. He was about to slip into synchrony with the near-dead Space Marine when the sound of a storm bolter firing resounded across his auto-senses. Several blurs of light on the auspex had detached themselves from the mass holding back, and were moving around the perimeter. Brother Santiago's report crackled over the vox.

'Two targets eliminated. Three more incoming.' Another, longer, burst of fire. 'Eliminated.'

The sensor readings showed other probing movements receding for the moment, moving back to the outer corridors and the decks above and below. Sergeant Dioneas stopped beside Calistarius.

'Scouting attacks. Let us hope that they do not realise our numbers are so small before the second wave arrives.'

Calistarius needed no further encouragement and crouched down with arm outstretched, his gauntleted fingers falling upon the bloodstained skin of Vespesario's forehead.

The ship itself tried to fight them as well as the daemons. Doorways appeared in solid walls and closed up again, separating the Blood Angels from each other. Vents in the shape of snarling mouths spewed clouds of flies that exploded like small incendiary shells. Metal decking melted underfoot, turning to a quagmire from which snapping tentacles and fanged maws erupted to drag down unfortunate legionaries.

They pressed on regardless, blasting and hewing their way through the daemonic assault, pushing ever onwards to the strategium where he knew the Arch-traitor would be found. They crossed impossible bridges over bottomless gulfs, battling red-skinned axe wielders with white eyes and bronze armour. They were assailed by multicoloured flames gouting from scything beasts that swooped down upon them from the heights of kilometre-long processional halls.

He knew that progress was slow, but there was something else at work. The interior of the Warmaster's battle-barge was like the inside of a warp breach, contorted and folded upon itself, a contained bubble of the immaterium far bigger than its external space.

There had to be something sustaining the breach, pouring warp energy into the real universe to uphold the diabolic structure and its daemon inhabitants.

Horus.

The Warmaster was a living portal, his superhuman body the only thing capable of transferring so much Chaos energy into the material realm. Not until the Warmaster was slain would they be freed.

As if this thought prompted a response, the Blood Angels, now numbering only six warriors, were confronted by warriors of the Traitor's Legion. Bolt and plasma converged upon them from galleries and mezzanines, forcing them to return to the winding passageways they had just left, where daemons waited with sickle blades and paralysing tongues.

Undeterred, he carved a path through his foes, borne forward not by hate or rage, but the desire to save his sons from this perverted torment.

They fight their way to the upper decks, advancing purposefully into the heart of the enemy, securing bulkheads and blast doors to seal off the foe's lines of attack. It is a folly to hope that they can achieve anything meaningful, but they are Space Marines, Blood Angels, sons of Sanguinius, and they will fight to their last breath. Cleanse and purge. Kill the alien. Suffer not the xenos to live. The main bridge may be their objective but extermination is their true goal.

They fire their storm bolters in short, controlled bursts, conserving ammunition as much as they can. The sergeants have their power swords, cutting down any genestealer that survives the hail of fire. Brother Geraneos has a heavy flamer. Blasts of super-hot promethium clear whole chambers of foes, the incendiary fuel a barrier to further attack, buying scant respite to reload and redistribute ammunition.

Cercanto, Rabellio, Zervantes and Desarius are dead. There is

*no thought of recovering their ancient battleplate, but their spare
magazines do not go to waste.*

*The foe withdraw from the advance, but none of the Blood Angels
mistake this for victory. The genestealers are not mindless animals,
that much has been learnt in previous campaigns. They possess
patience and cunning, guided by a psychic gestalt for the near flaw-
less coordination of attacks. The Blood Angels' foes are waiting, biding
their time while the Terminators traverse the open galleries and broad
storage halls of the third and fourth deck; there are few crawl ducts
and hiding spaces from which to launch an ambush. Perhaps they
know that the Space Marines are heading for the controls in the
bridge and are saving their numbers for a last overwhelming defence.*

*The Blood Angels take stock, pausing for a few seconds in one
of the long mess halls that run nearly four hundred metres along
the spine of the ship. The number of rusted benches and tables
riveted to the floor suggest that the ship must have housed thousands of crew. A few lighting strips still work, powered by some
auxiliary system, flickering dismal yellow in patches, creating shadows that dance with their own life.*

*'Not to sound overly optimistic, brothers, but I think we might
have a chance,' says Serrajo. 'I've studied the sensorium readings
and I think the enemy number in their hundreds, not thousands.'*

*To most warriors such news would be cold comfort – hundreds of
genestealers against half a dozen seems impossible odds – but to the
Blood Angels of the First Company this is greeted with cautious hope.*

*'A small infestation,' says Sergeant Commeos. 'You are right,
we might yet survive this encounter.'*

*'We have a small group moving on the right flank.' Lucasi's
warning turns the ad-hoc squad in time to see figures scuttling
through the broken mess doors. To the surprise of the Space
Marines, lasbeams and bullets zip and whine out of the darkness towards them.*

The figures spilling into the hall are a contortion of human form, hunched and misshapen as though made of wax and left near a flame. Some have extra eyes, while others sport additional flailing, jointless arms. Many are disfigured with protruding spines and haphazard growths of serrated chitin.

Unlike the purestrain genestealers they carry weapons. Inaccurate fire patters on the Terminators' armour and the tables nearby as the Space Marines move to respond, their storm bolters throwing a hail of rounds into the incoming mass of degenerate half-breeds.

'Hybrids,' snarls Adonius. 'Wipe them out.'

Shotguns boom and autoguns rattle in response as the Terminators close on their foes, their tactical dreadnought armour designed to withstand anti-tank rounds and artillery bombardments. Power gloves smash bones and crush limbs as the crippled hybrids throw themselves ineffectually at the Emperor's chosen. Vespesario swings his fist without relent, pulping skulls and mashing internal organs.

Suddenly a white-blue bolt of energy screams across the hall, catching Commeos on the side of the helm. The plasma explodes in a detonation of raw energy, turning the sergeant's head into an expanding cloud of vaporised liquid and tissue.

A lascannon bolt slices through the bulkhead close at hand, narrowly missing Serrajo.

'Back,' orders Adonius, turning his storm bolter onto the new arrivals.

There are too few of them to risk losing a warrior to the hybrids' heavier weaponry and they retreat from the mess hall, covering their withdrawal with a continuous stream of bolts.

Retracting his mind from the whorl of Vespesario's thoughts, Calistarius passed on this vital piece of intelligence.

'Those are not scouting attacks,' responded Dioneas. 'The genestealers are attempting to lock us into position while their hybrids bring heavy weapons to bear. The tactical situation is not improving, Brother-Lexicanium. We need a mobile defence or we will make easy targets.'

'A minute, no longer,' Calistarius told him. 'I have almost found out what happened to the previous boarding party. I sense that if I can locate his memories of what happened on the main bridge we shall know what we are facing.'

'Sixty seconds, no more.'

Calistarius nodded and focused his thoughts. There was no more time for subtlety, exploring Vespesario's thoughts as though sifting through wreckage. If the Librarian were to discover what had occurred two centuries ago he needed to find it swiftly. The extension of his thoughts into the other Blood Angel became a lance of burning energy, drilling down through Vespesario's psyche into the pulsing core of his memories, shredding everything else in the vicinity. After the Black Rage and so long in suspended animation, Vespesario no longer possessed anything close to a rational mind that would be destroyed by the intrusion. Only good grace had stopped Calistarius being so blunt before.

Growling and snarling, feeling the Black Rage seeping into his soul, Calistarius opened himself up to the weight of Vespesario's experiences, allowing everything to flood in. Fighting against the tide of pain and anger, the Librarian ripped free what he needed, raw and bleeding like a heart torn still beating from the chest.

The strategium. Darkness suffused the massive chamber, broken only by the hellish glimmer of daemon eyes and pulsing warp energy. Bathed in the actinic glow was the Warmaster, encased in battleplate fashioned from the artifice of lunatics and shaped by the whim of Dark Gods.

Horus held up his claws, brandishing them in a display of defiance.

Sword flashing, he hurled himself at the Traitor, ducking beneath a sweeping claw, blade outstretched. A glowing fist met the burning sword and sparks erupted, filling the darkness with a moment of blinding light.

He attacked again, and again was parried with a storm of lightning. Eluding a return blow, he lunged for the head but his sword was turned aside, ripping across armour plates, carving a white-hot furrow where it passed.

The Warmaster snarled and swept his claws upwards, raking agony across the chest of the Blood Angel. Staggering back, he half-warded away the Traitor's next blow, losing a shoulder pad to the slashing talons.

He threw himself aside to dodge the next assault, ignoring the burning in his lungs, the agonised thrashing of his heart.

The next attack came not from the Traitor's claws but his mind. Psychic energy flared, coruscating through the darkness to hurl the Blood Angel across the strategium. Fronds of sable energy crackled over his armour, scratching and stinging like a million wasps.

Worse still, the Warmaster's thoughts were inside his head, threatening and cajoling, daring him to fight, demanding his surrender.

He could be immortal, Horus promised, if he would only swear his allegiance to a new master. There was nothing to be gained by this pointless resistance. A painful death was no reward for so many centuries of service.

The promise was an affront to all that he held dear. The idea that the Warmaster thought he was capable of being swayed by such argument was too much. Fuelled by a sudden rage he lashed out, his thoughts hurling back the psychic attack, his sword piercing Horus's side.

The Traitor's scream was mixed with demented laughter, a howl of victory as much as pain.

It was then that he realised he would fail if he fought. His sons would perish and all those he had sworn to protect would be consumed by the warp-spawned madness that had been unleashed.

The rage wanted him to fight. The hatred was boiling in his veins, urging him to slash and stab and rend this vile mockery of the man he had once called brother. But he could not give in to the anger, could not submit himself to the vengeance of mindless violence. There was a deeper truth that had to be protected.

He threw himself into the darkness, letting it consume him, the icy chill of the abyss freezing his lungs, setting a chill in his veins, numbing his thoughts until he was part of the darkness itself.

Calistarius struggled, the sacrifice of Vespesario sending a surge of memory into him, breaking like a shard of ice in his thoughts, filling him with a single imperative: slay the Traitor!

Reeling away from Vespesario, Calistarius barely noticed the final glimmer of life had fled the Blood Angel's body. With his last measure of vitality the Terminator had sent his final warning.

'The main bridge!' Calistarius barked. He switched to the command channel. 'Captain Raphael. You must despatch the second wave immediately!'

'Explain yourself, Brother-Librarian,' snapped Sergeant Dioneas as Calistarius exited the chamber and set off along the corridor. 'What did you see?'

'A trap, brother-sergeant. A terrible, beguiling trap.'

Slamming his fist into the vestiges of the bridge door, Vespesario opens a hole wide enough to step through. Behind him Sergeant

Adonius's storm bolter roars for a few more seconds as he cuts down another genestealer attack.

Pushing his way onto the main bridge, Vespesario finds himself in near-total darkness, the only light a few blinking indicators on a panel to his right and a red haze from a broken viewscreen ahead. His armour's auto-senses flash through alternatives to the usual spectrum, strobing his view for a half-second before settling on thermal register. Even so it takes a few more seconds for him to realise all is not right with the console beneath the shattered plate of the central display screen.

Twists of cables and snaking wires form a constricting web around something entirely organic. It is hard to discern where mechanical and biological meet, but in the grey shades of cool air he notices that what he took for corrugated tubing is in fact ribbed flesh, sheathed in a segment of black chitin. Above is a nodule that he interprets as an elbow and a flare of carapace over the shoulder.

Though some of its bulk is lost in the mess of machinery, it is easily twice as large as the Terminator. Two human-like arms slowly flex back and forth, tri-fingered hands opening and closing with dormant menace, while the lower set of the torso append-ages are tiny, fidgeting digits no bigger than two fingers pressed together, tipped with a slender claw. More chitin covers the chest and abdomen, haphazard with random nodules and aberrant wart-like clusters of malformed hard tissue.

He drags his eyes to the bulging, monstrous head, larger than any creature's he has seen before. More cables intersect with ichor-dribbling apertures, either side of a ridge of flanges run-ning along the crest of the scalp. The mouth hangs open limply, fangs stunted and blunt, but the eyes that open slowly to regard him with malign alien intelligence are all too familiar.

It is almost too much to understand, so far outside his experience, so far from expected behaviour that he doubts his own senses for a moment. Vespesario struggles to find answers for the questions that crowd his thoughts. It is a collision of opposites, of the feral nature of the genestealer and the artisanship of the Cult Mechanicus. Hybrids bearing weapons is one thing, a fully grown genestealer patriarch meshed with human technology is something entirely different.

There is something else, something so far out of place that he had disregarded it at first.

A third eye splits the forehead of the monstrous half-mechanical genestealer. He meets its gaze for a moment and time loses all meaning.

Like ash ascending on the smoke of a pyre he is lifted up, swept from his weak body into the embrace of a loving god. Brotherhood and belonging, duty and sacrifice, these are values the brood understand. These are virtues to them.

The brood survives, and he will survive with the brood. Others will come, others like the first that were taken and others like him. They will come to be part of the brood also and know the infinite satisfaction of belonging.

It has happened before and will happen again. Timeless, the brood continues, luring in the curious and the dutiful, taking them unto itself to sustain the brood for another generation.

Vespesario has feared nothing since he survived the deserts and came to the people of the Blood. Not death on the battlefield, not injury or torment. Bodily dread is impossible to him, but as he witnesses the eternal life of the brood, leeching its life from those it traps, using them to steer it to more victims, he is filled with a far more existential fear.

The Omen of Despair is no itinerant threat, no random visitor to worlds and systems, deposited by the vagaries of the warp. There is purpose behind its peregrination. It moves with a will, guided by the bloated creature that rules the brood, a far superior creature to any mere genestealer patriarch. This ship, the heart of the space hulk, provided something new and invigorating, something that altered the genetics and the destiny of the genestealers that had come aboard.

The third eye is all the evidence required, proof of the obscene nature of the brood's interbreeding for a dozen generations and more.

The Navigator's eye, a genetic mutation bred into the Navigator Houses during the Dark Age of Technology so that they could look upon the warp itself and steer a ship. Those genestrains bred into the aliens again and again through new human hosts, attempting to perfect with random mutation what ancient Terra's scientists had constructed in laboratories, and given final form in the navigator-patriarch.

For centuries it has moved across the galaxy, emerging from the warp using the resonance of humanity's thoughts, guided to populated worlds and drifting starships, dropping back into the warp to trap aboard those who have come to investigate and conquer. An ancient ship, a treasure vault of archeotech and lost knowledge so powerful that not even the Blood Angels would destroy it out of hand. The perfect guise, the perfect lure for adepts of the Machine God, Ecclesiarchy missionaries, Imperial servants of all ranks and divisions, ensnared by the false promise of glory and bounty.

Worse still is the glimpse of the future, the desired path of the Omen of Despair, its ultimate destination arrived at from the desires and memories of a hundred thousand victims of the brood. A planet teeming with life, billions upon billions, and at its heart a mind so powerful that it broadcasts a beacon across the galaxy. The Astronomican, light of the Emperor, the guiding path followed by Navigators for ten thousand years, entrenched into the most fundamental genetics of the brood, an imperative that drives everything they do.

A return home. To Terra.

To be one with the creator-Emperor.

The sensation fills Vespesario, fulfilling every desire, his own gene-seed aching to be united with the primogenitor, the Master of Mankind. The brood feels it too, the bond singing like a choir in their minds, calling him to come with them, to guide them to the paradise they seek.

The thought terrifies him. It terrifies Vespesario in a way that no mortal danger ever could. The idea that he might bring this unholy infection to the doors of Terra itself fills him with a grief and dread so grave that if he could have willed himself dead at that moment his hearts would have stopped.

And greater still is the fear that he will not be able to fight the urge much longer, the knowledge that he will succumb. A physical foe he can face, but a psychic attack will eventually wear down even the defences of a Space Marine.

In reaction to this hopelessness, rage erupts. A rage burned into the gene-seed he carries, a psychic after-echo of a disastrous fate that still echoes down the millennia. The rage gives him strength, shattering the bond of the patriarch-navigator, granting him a moment's clarity as battle-hormones surge through his system in unprecedented quantity, awakening every cell in his body to the latent strength encoded within.

The brood recoils from the gene-rage, sickened by its touch.

He has but a moment and strikes, firing his storm bolter to gouge a wound in the patriarch's flank. It is not enough, not nearly enough to slay such a beast, but he senses that it is all he has the strength remaining to do.

It is not enough to die here. Like moths to a flame, others will be drawn to the space hulk, feeding the brood's gene-hunger for another generation, bringing the Omen of Despair *a few more light years closer to the heart of the Imperium, a grotesque spider in the guise of a resplendent butterfly.*

The rage gives him strength to fight the brood but duty, honour, sacrifice, these are the qualities that bolster the courage he needs to run, to flee, to protect himself so that he might carry a warning.

Adonius is dead at the door but the brood do not attack when he emerges, still confused by the conflicting psychic signals and pain emanating from their patriarch. Vespesario breaks into a lumbering run, heading into the depths of the ship, closing doors and bulkheads behind him, forestalling pursuit until even he does not know where he is.

His wounds are great. Only the madness of the Black Rage sustains him, and he knows that his sanity will not last much longer. He wants to turn and face his foes, to cut them down with storm bolter and rip them apart with his power fist.

A deeper goal flares inside, just long enough to find the small magazine chamber, just long enough to open the locks and step inside the closing door, breaking the mechanism to seal himself into a living tomb. He hears them scratching and battering the door but the ammunition storage cell is designed to withstand starship bombardments. On the verge of death he waits, praying for calm, for peace, and for the strength to survive.

And the cold comes as his life leeches away, hearts slowing, breaths becoming shallower, the sus-an membrane flooding his system, becoming one with the rage and hatred, sealing the truth inside a coffin of flesh.

With Calistarius leading the charge, the Blood Angels punched through the gathering genestealers. The aliens had not been expecting an attack and were caught unawares by the sudden offensive. Spurred on by desperation, Calistarius hurled psychic blasts as much as he used his pistol and sword, incinerating the genestealers. The storm bolters of his brethren finished off the survivors of the psychic assault.

'Why do we not wait for the second wave?' asked Sergeant Dioneas.

'As soon as reinforcements land, the navigator-beast will activate the warp engines.'

'So why did you call them in?' the sergeant demanded. 'Have you not doomed the whole company?'

'I am sure the creature knows we are just a scouting force. If it judges we are going to leave, I think it will simply take us into the warp. It must be able to detect the incoming boarding torpedoes and so it will wait. We have to kill it before they arrive.'

'If we fail?'

'You must send the abort signal before the second wave makes contact. They must not set foot on the *Omen of Despair* or we shall all be lost. Better that we are taken than the whole of the First Company.'

'That is a terrible gamble, brother, I hope you know what to do.'

Calistarius said nothing, but the piece of memory stuck in his mind from Vespesario was more than enough to give him confidence.

The truth lay in delusions, oddly enough. Everything Vespesario had witnessed, everything he had experienced on board the *Omen of Despair* had been translated into his rage-fevered hallucinations as Lord Sanguinius.

A febrile creation, not memories at all.

The Librarian could feel its presence even now, lingering in a corner of his mind like a smouldering ember, ready to ignite again if he gave it a chance. For most the Black Rage was a curse but for Calistarius and his companions it had become a blessing, the last chance for Vespesario to give them his warning two centuries after his doom.

'Get me to the bridge, that is our only objective,' the Librarian told his battle-brothers. Dioneas was content to comply, despatching the squad to create a breach-head around the command deck. It took several minutes to push back the lingering genestealers with storm bolter and flamer, but eventually the cordon was secure enough for Calistarius to make his last move.

The door of the bridge was still rent asunder from Vespesario's attacks. Calistarius hardened his thoughts, both to the vile scene that awaited him and to the psychic attack that would surely come. He stepped over the threshold, sword at the ready, and confronted the genestealer patriarch.

It was even more horrendous than Vespesario's memories had conveyed. It had expanded, filling half the bridge now, disgusting sub-growths of soft flesh and chitin suspended by wires, sustained by pulsing feed tubes that filled the air with the stench of decay. Calistarius's olfactory filters were almost overwhelmed by it.

The third eye had become a semi-autonomous appendage, jutting from the bloated face of the patriarch on a long stalk, pierced by clips and hooks linked by coiled cables to the warp engine console.

The eye swung toward Calistarius even as the navigator-patriarch's clawed hands reached for him. Rather than trying to avoid its otherworldly stare he met the alien's gaze full-on, allowing the Black Rage of Vespesario's memories to flow forth.

He felt the same timeless void of the brood, as old as the stars, impossibly distant and ancient, reborn through a million generations since a beginning in another galaxy, the tiniest fragment of a much greater whole yearning to be reunited, forever devoured by inner emptiness.

The rage boiled up inside him and he seized hold of the psychic connection, pouring wrath and scorn into his foe without relent.

Psychically and physically the patriarch thrashed to break free, emitting an unearthly wail as ten thousand years of grief and desire for vengeance were made manifest in its mind. It burned like fire, turning alien intelligence to ash, searing through the hypnotic lure of the brood, leaping from one genestealer to the next like a plague, infecting their thoughts with alien anger and hatred so intense that they fell upon each other in their desire to rend and kill.

Claws as hard as titanium closed on his armour, cracking ceramite, puncturing fibre bundles, pushing closer and closer to his gene-enhanced flesh and bones.

He saw not a bizarre hybrid of alien and machine but the very image of treachery – the thrice-cursed Warmaster, Horus the Betrayer, the Architect of Ruin. Calistarius lunged as Sanguinius had lunged, reincarnated as the Lord of the Blood Angels, the Saviour of Baal.

His sword passed into the wound caused by Vespesario's storm bolter, sliding deep into the patriarch's innards, parting nerve bundles and piercing its pulmonary organs.

With a last twitch of muscle the patriarch tossed Calistarius across the bridge. The Librarian lost his grip on his sword, leaving it lodged in the thorax of the alien monster. Ichor spewed from the wound, splashing onto the deck, bubbling with escaping air.

The patriarch-navigator's third eye flopped to its face, the psychic light within dimming to nothing. Its chest collapsed with a wheeze of expulsed breath, and it fell still.

* * *

In disarray at the loss of their brood-leader, the genestealers were easy prey for the vengeful Blood Angels. Calistarius was content to let the First Company purge the *Omen of Despair* and allowed himself to be escorted back to the breaching zone by Sergeant Dioneas.

'I would think you would be in a more celebratory mood,' the sergeant said as they arrived at the outer perimeter and were met by an Apothecary and a Techmarine ready to tend their wounds and damaged armour.

'I'm tired, very tired,' explained Calistarius.

It was true. He felt a fatigue the like of which he had never known before, drawn out by physical exertion, psychic combat and, most of all, the harrowing ordeal of sharing Vespesario's Black Rage-induced warp-memories.

But it was more than exhaustion that quietened Calistarius. Something altogether more disturbing occupied his thoughts. It was a moment, a passing vision that had entered his mind at the instant he had unleashed the Black Rage into the thoughts of the patriarch. He was not sure if it were one of Vespesario's cursed hallucinations, an actual memory from the Terminator's ordeal two hundred years before, or something else far more dangerous: a glimpse of something yet to happen.

His instinct told him it was the latter.

For a fraction of a second, Calistarius had felt himself entombed, buried in a vast mausoleum, gripped by a terrible thirst for blood, shrieking for release, enslaved to the curse of the Black Rage.

ABOUT THE AUTHORS

Gav Thorpe is the author of the Primarchs novel *Lorgar: Bearer of the Word*, the Horus Heresy novels *Deliverance Lost*, *Angels of Caliban* and *Corax*, as well as the novella *The Lion*, which formed part of the *New York Times* bestselling collection *The Primarchs*, and several audio dramas. He has written many novels for Warhammer 40,000, including *Ashes of Prospero*, *Imperator: Wrath of the Omnissiah* and *Rise of the Ynnari: Ghost Warrior*. For Warhammer, Gav has penned the End Times novel *The Curse of Khaine*, the Warhammer Chronicles trilogy *The Sundering*, and much more besides. In 2017, Gav received the David Gemmell Legend Award for his Age of Sigmar novel *Warbeast*. He lives and works in Nottingham.

YOUR NEXT READ

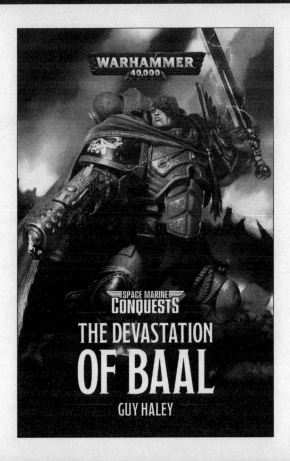

WARHAMMER 40,000

SPACE MARINE CONQUESTS

THE DEVASTATION
OF BAAL

GUY HALEY

THE DEVASTATION OF BAAL
Guy Haley

Baal is besieged! The alien horror of Hive Fleet Leviathan has reached the Blood
Angels' home world, and their entire existence is under threat. As the sons of
Sanguinius gather, the battle for the fate of their bloodline begins…

Find this title, and many others, on blacklibrary.com and in all good bookshops